ASHLEY BEEGAN

The Revelation

First edition

This book was professionally typeset on Reedsy.
Find out more at reedsy.com

Contents

1

Swanson

Despite the sweat that covered his body, Detective Inspector Alex Swanson sucked in another lungful of the biting December air. The tallest peak of the hike was close by, and his chest begged for a break, but he leaned forward and forced his aching feet upwards to the stone cairn of the Peak District hill known as Grindslow Knoll.

The route from Edale wouldn't usually cause such painful feet, and he cursed himself for wearing new walking boots. Hart was right; it was definitely the wrong decision. Not that he'd ever admit that to her gloating face.

Grindslow Knoll sat at the western side of Grindsbook Clough in the highest and wildest area of the Peak District - the Dark Peak. It was so named after the soil, but there was an unusually dark atmosphere about when he reached the cairn. He stopped to take a breath, hands on his hips, and scanned the view of the frost-bound Kinder Scout to the north. It was great that the weather hadn't turned too wintery yet. The lack of rain so far this year meant the ground, plus the general visibility, was not bad at all for December. Yet the ominous feeling continued to tingle his skin as he relished the view.

There were no clouds in the sky, which made the slight breeze bitingly icy at six hundred metres in the air. It was certainly below zero. Not many people were equipped to handle the cold as well as Swanson, which made the rolling hills of the Derbyshire peaks quieter in winter. He'd passed a few tough hikers but not many. There'd been possibly ten of others dispersed at various intervals, and they'd been mostly of the older generation. They were much hardier than most people Swanson knew his own age or younger.

Not that it bothered him. The solidarity was the best thing about hiking alone. It was the only space that gave him the chance to think calmly and without interruption. He expanded all of his focus and energy on getting through the hike. Walking always gave him his best ideas so he could think through any problems—mainly work-related stuff. It was a natural sedative. But the pit of dread in his stomach wasn't going anywhere today.

It had been embarrassing to realise he'd left both of his phones in the car a third of the way up the Grindsbrook Clough. Such a novice thing to do when hiking alone. But the ominous feeling that crept through his bones might be just that. The lack of being able to communicate should he want to. Wasn't that a lot of people's worst fear?

Or something dreadful was waiting for him to come back and retrieve it.

He climbed down the hill and followed the bitter Grindsbrook Booth back to Edale. It was lunchtime by the time he arrived back at the car park, which was twice as busy as it had been at 7 a.m. It pleased him to see no one had yet parked next to his beloved black Audi, which he'd carefully parked in the furthest corner from the entrance.

When he reached the vehicle, he could see his work phone sitting proudly on the passenger seat for anyone to see. He was lucky no one had smashed his window and stolen the damn thing. Despite the feeling of something important waiting for him, he delayed checking the notifications and ignored the phone as he pulled on a fresh T-shirt, socks, and trainers from the boot of the car.

He lit his second cigarette of the day and took a few deep drags before finally opening the passenger door and giving in to the feeling of dread. Four missed calls flashed up. Two from Rebecca Hart, one from Summer Thomas, and one from the ice queen boss, Jane Murray. His gut feeling was right, then. Something had kicked off if Murray was looking for him as well as Hart and Summer. He opened up a text from Hart.

Body. Call me.

Of course it had to be a body. Hart was not usually a person of so few words. Especially so few curse words. His finger hovered over the Call button, but he waited until the very last drag of his cigarette before calling her. She answered on the second ring.

"Finally. It's been hours. I thought you were bloody dead," she snapped dramatically.

He grinned at her familiar annoyance. "Of course I'm not dead. Be careful, though. I might start to think you care about me if you keep acting like this. Hello to you too, by the way."

"Whatever. Where have you been gallivanting around this time?"

He could practically see her throwing her arms around as she spoke, and the low hum of conversation in the background informed him she was already in the office. It wouldn't surprise him if she'd spent the first morning of her weekend working.

"Edale. It is Saturday. It's my day off, you know? I'm allowed to gallivant wherever I like. Even *outside* of Derbyshire, should I wish to."

"It was supposed to be my day off too, but not anymore. Someone found a body and Murray wants you and me on it ASAP. Are you still there?"

He lost his grin and sighed deeply, disappointed she paid no heed to his bait and ruined his peaceful morning anyway. "In Edale? Yes, I'm still here. Why?"

"I need you to get to Ilkeston. The body is there. It's a lady who looks to be around fifty years old. No ID yet." She hesitated. "She's in Bell Woods."

"Bell Woods?" Every part of his body was suddenly on full alert. "Is this something to do with . . . what we found there in summer?"

There was a pause before Hart responded. If it was something to do with the summer's events then she would not take it well.

"Billy Bailey and Marcie Livingstone?" she said finally. "Or our dear friend Charlie Marsh?"

"Well, yes. Any of them, I suppose."

"No. It's a fresh body and they're all dead or locked up. She's been dead for twenty-four hours at most, so it can't be anything to do with the last set of bodies we found. A couple of officers are already there. Leave now and I'll see you there in an hour."

The line went dead. Swanson cursed as he threw the phone back on to the front seat. He thought he'd seen the last of Bell bloody Woods. Which was quite a fitting name for the place considering how many bodies they'd found this year. Now there was another secret to uncover, and to top it off, he was nearly fifty miles away.

He sighed as he strapped in and set off to Edale Road. By the time he'd reached the M1 from the Heath Interchange, the peace that had temporarily stilled his mind had disappeared completely. Instead, dead bodies and motives for murder filled his mind, along with flashes of Charlie Marsh's pained screams as she burned alive in front of him to protect them all from her own sister—the deranged serial killer known as Marcie Livingstone.

2

Swanson

Swanson couldn't stop the memories of Charlie Marsh's death as he drove towards Ilkeston. Even six months after her tragic death she entered his thoughts often, and like every other time he was overcome with a feeling that he could've done more to save her. He could've rushed forward. They could have reached the house ten minutes earlier. Even five minutes would've made all the difference in the world to Marsh. She'd be alive. Livingstone would be in prison. Not that he could mention either name in Hart's presence without her getting huffy. It was too painful for her after what she'd shared with Marsh.

The only one of the sibling trio still alive was Billy Bailey. Since the others were six feet under, he was the only one who the Crown Prosecution Service, or CPS, could prosecute for all the murders. But Bailey lost his mind when he was told his sisters were gone. It wasn't clear if he had a grasp of his mental health in the first place, but he certainly no longer had any control of it after his sisters died.

Police Constable Lisa Trent had been the one to tell Bailey

about his sisters. She said he screamed horrifically at Marsh's death, but shut down into a completely catatonic state when he then heard of Marcie Livingstone's death. He now lived in a secure mental health facility and as far as Swanson knew, he hadn't spoken a word to anyone in six months.

He wouldn't even speak to Summer anymore, the resident forensic psychologist for Derbyshire Police. She was the only person he'd speak to when he first tried to confess to his crimes. So the full story was something that niggled at Swanson. It was as though he'd completed a 1,000 piece jigsaw and found out at the end there was a piece missing. The darkest piece that was so small its absence wasn't immediately obvious to anyone who simply skimmed the puzzle. It looked complete from a distance. But he could see the gap, and he knew Hart hadn't told him everything Marsh had said to her.

It took ninety minutes to reach Bell Woods in the end. Other officers had already blocked off the entrance with police tape, and he could see Summer's mum's house as he pulled up on the side of the busy main road. She lived on the adjacent street. He considered parking on her drive to keep his car off the main road. Their relationship had come a long way since he first met her whilst looking for an escaped mental health patient who, according to officials, didn't actually exist. But that would mean dodging lots of questions about what was happening in the woods, and it was hard to say no to your possible future mother-in-law. So he decided the main road would be fine.

Hart was already there, which was no surprise as she only lived down the road from Ilkeston. She leant against her red Mini, but stepped forward when she saw him and tightened up the dark trench coat that covered her body almost in full. It was probably supposed to be knee-length. She was just short with an attitude to match. Like a Chihuahua.

She watched him as he parked up. He could swear the signature bob that framed her face was darker than usual. Maybe she'd had her hair done this weekend. Or it seemed that way because of the angry glare she was giving him.

"You decided to turn up at last, then?" she called as he exited the car.

"You're delightful today, aren't you?" he replied.

He gently closed the car door and strolled towards her as he took in the surrounding scene. Bell Woods was fairly small, but thanks to the overhanging trees above, the entrance was dark and foreboding. Officers and forensic staff were already walking around. Those white suits made any place look creepy.

He assessed the wide entrance he already knew well. It was easy to drive into with a body in the boot. The overhanging trees meant the vehicle would disappear from the street view pretty quickly. The woods were usually pretty quiet at night too. Apart from teenagers getting drunk at the weekend. Hart was still frowning at him when he reached her.

"What's wrong?" he asked.

"Nothing," she snapped. "Other than someone finding a body on my day off and then having to wait around for you before I can do anything."

"I got here as quickly as I could. Have you had your hair done?"

"No. Why?" Her hand instantly went to smooth her already perfect hair.

It was just her bad mood after all, then. Or the lack of sun.

"No reason. It looks good. What have we got here then?" The pair walked under the thorny branches of the ancient oak trees that darkened the entrance. It was nearly 3 p.m., and the sky was already growing dim.

"A local jogger found the body of a woman who looks to be around fifty years old. Someone hid her off the main path - but not too far off it. Whoever was involved didn't hide the body very well. Either they didn't care if someone found it, or they got interrupted and ran off in a hurry."

"How do we know someone is involved? Maybe it's natural causes," Swanson replied.

"They have stabbed her at least three times."

"Fair enough," Swanson muttered. "That's pretty suspicious."

They continued on the wide, man-made path that ran through the middle of the woods. The concrete path was outlined by a wooden fence on either side that was only about two feet high with occasional gaps to allow easy access to the woodland. Enormous trees grew on either side of the path, their stark branches reaching out above as if searching for each other.

Swanson's stepdad had always insisted trees were watching everything around them. He said they had memories. And that might have been the only thing he and his stepdad ever agreed on. The way the trees in Bell Woods reached out for each other looked as though they were in mourning for the atrocities life had forced them to bear witness to.

A few metres into the woods, someone had placed another police cordon blocking off a path to the right. One officer stood guard at the fence with his hands behind his back. The dark police uniform swallowed up his skinny frame, and pimples surrounded his grim expression. Hart's elbow dug sharply into Swanson's ribs.

"Look," she whispered. Or at least she thought she did. She

wasn't the best at whispering. "It's another one of those child officers you keep going on about."

She fell quiet when they reached the tape, but she was right. One thing he'd noticed about reaching his mid-thirties was that sometimes adults with proper jobs looked like children. They *were* children. And he wasn't sure he'd ever get used to it.

He flashed his ID to the kid and swung his leg over the fence. The natural light became even more sparse as he trod gently between the tree trunks and deeper into the woodland, with Hart's footsteps not too far behind his own. The floor of the woodland itself was well-walked. The thousands of footsteps that had made their way through the trees over the years had forced narrow paths to form in between the trees for Swanson to follow easily.

The ground was strangely soft underfoot to say the rain had been sparse that autumn. It would probably harden with the forecast of icy days ahead. The only flowers that seemed to have survived the winter so far were some creamy yellow primrose clustered low to the ground, though the air carried an earthy scent mixed with damp and rotting vegetation.

"Smells like pine cones in here," Hart mused.

"I disagree," Swanson replied and wrinkled his nose against the smell of decay. The fresh air of the Peak District hills was now a distant memory, though his feet still ached, but that smell was one he much preferred.

It didn't take long to find the spot where the body had been found. Several people, some in uniform and some in suits, gathered around a deep dip in the ground. One of them had erected a white shelter already, and next to it was a man with a puffy face and large middle who was almost the same height as Swanson. He stood next to the tent with his arms folded and wore a grim look.

"There's the SOCO." Hart nodded towards the man, or the Scene of Crime Officer as he was more formally known. Swanson had met the guy a few times during other incidents, and always remembered his charmingly grumpy nature.

"What's his name again?" Swanson asked in a low voice. "Jim?"

"Bloody hell, Swanson. It's Jeremy Smith," Hart tutted. "How do you never remember names?"

He shrugged his enormous shoulders. "I was close enough."

They moved towards the SOCO. A thin twig snapped under Swanson's foot and Jeremy's head snapped up. He put his hand up like a school crossing patrol's *Stop* sign. The pair froze, and he glowered with tired eyes as he trod over to them.

"Jeremy," Hart said with a nod of her head when he approached.

"All right? Not much scene preservation going on here," he grumbled as he looked down at their unprotected feet.

Jeremy was pushing retirement, and made it clear he'd had enough of the job at every scene. Swanson stifled back a grin. He liked the guy's attitude. Jeremy put it straight no matter who you were, and Swanson couldn't help but admire that.

"It's always hard to protect a woodland scene, eh," Hart replied.

"Mm." Jeremy folded his arms once more. "Murray said you two would give me a visit. What do you know so far?"

"A jogger has found the body of a woman," Swanson replied. "She's thought to be around fifty years old. Someone has stabbed her three times. That's it."

"At *least* three times," Jeremy replied. "Personally, I think it was much more. I think it was someone in a frenzy judging from the state of her. Then they dumped her here. We don't know who she is yet. They dumped her on her side, fully clothed. No evidence of sexual assault so far. They dragged her from that direction looking at the marks on the ground."

He pointed to the far side of the tent where someone had set up even more police cordon.

"That would suggest she didn't walk into the woods the same way we did then. There's CCTV on the main road. If someone drove her here in a car to dump the body·, we'll be able to see it," Swanson said. "Or they know the place well and got inside another way. Is there another entrance?"

"Yes. An officer looked around and there's a farm at that end which has a private road leading to it from the end of the main path." He pointed to the opposite end to which Swanson and Hart had entered the woods and then pointed behind them. "And over there is a field which leads on to a housing estate where the old adventure theme park used to be. I don't think there's anything there other than the housing estate these days. Such a shame."

"Everything is a housing estate these days," Swanson muttered.

"Yep, those damn investors ruin everything. I used to take my kids to that theme park. Bloody idiots ran it into the ground then sold it off and filled their pockets. Anyway, behind me is the main road you would've driven on. That's full of houses which back on to the edge of the woods."

"Creepy." Hart made a face.

"But the direction in which the drag marks come from is the farm?" Swanson asked.

Jeremy nodded. "We also found some footprints near the drag marks. They'll still be in the tent by the way. You won't be able to see the body anytime soon. My main report will be ready by tomorrow. Stay on this side when you're looking around, though. I really would like to preserve as much as possible."

Swanson nodded and stepped away from them both to take in the scene. It was a miserable place to die. Or to be correct, it was a miserable place to be dragged through by your murderer and then abandoned. It was dark and lonely, and probably not somewhere most people would want to be left alone whether they were alive or dead. Summer grew up near these woods. She'd once been chased by someone who had run away from the psych ward of the nearby hospital. Her and her little brother had to run all the way home to get away.

Maybe Charlie Marsh had it better than this poor lady. One painful blaze of glory and she was gone, cleansed of her sins and remembered as a hero. It was a literal baptism of fire. Maybe her screams were worth it. Maybe he could one day do the same.

3

Summer

Summer Thomas smiled as familiar voices floated down the corridor towards the small kitchen in the station. She often heard Swanson and Hart arguing before she could see either of them. Sometimes it was Swanson's familiar grunt and Hart's unmistakable high heel stomping that gave them away first. She popped her head around the doorway and watched them as they headed her way.

"How can it be anything to do with Billy Bailey?" Hart said, throwing her hands in the air in frustration.

Summer's curiosity piqued at the mention of Billy Bailey. She'd spent many hours trying to get him to talk after what happened to Charlie Marsh. He'd never so much as raised his gaze at her, keeping his empty eyes firmly on the table instead.

"I'm just saying it's worth asking him the question," Swanson replied to Hart calmly.

"Billy Bailey hasn't spoken a word in months, Swanson. Not even to Summer. Do you have a magic wand to wave which will cure him and make him talk to us? No." Hart looked up and spotted Summer watching them. "Oh hi, Summer. You will make this idiot boyfriend of yours see sense."

"Hi, Hart," Summer replied.

She gave Swanson a wide smile, and in return he gave her a sort of half-smile half-grunt. Which was really his own version of a wide smile. They had a no-affection-in-the-office rule, which was hard when he looked so damn good in jeans. She noticed his eyes flicker over her own outfit appreciatively and forced her attention to Hart. She would not prove Murray right about workforce relationships being distracting.

"Why are you talking about Billy Bailey?" Summer stepped backwards into the kitchen to let the pair walk past her. As usual, Hart went straight to the kettle for her life source: coffee. Swanson grabbed a can of Fanta Lemon from the fridge.

"Swanson here wants to do your job. He thinks he's got special powers and *he's* the one to finally make Bailey talk again," Hart explained once she'd brimmed the kettle and flicked it on, causing the ancient appliance to grumble as if it was about to blow them all up.

"You think you can do better than me, do you?" Summer teased. "I didn't realise you'd completed seven years of psychological training at uni too."

"That's not what I said at all." Swanson groaned and placed his can of pop down on the table that sat in the middle of the room. "I was actually wanting to speak to *you* about it, Summer. Our very own expert. As you've just pointed out."

"Go ahead." Summer gestured, feeling one of his special favour requests coming on. She leaned back against the kitchen counter with her arms crossed.

"We could do with a favour," Swanson said tentatively.

"How did I know you were going to say that?" She grinned. "What's the favour this time then?"

15

"You're going to make me say it, aren't you?" He sighed. "Let me explain first. There's been a body found in one of the same areas that Bailey directed us to in the summer."

"Which place is it in?" Summer asked, her grin gone. "That house in Long Eaton?"

"No." He paused and gazed up at her. She knew what he was going to say before he even confirmed it. "Bell Woods."

Summer muttered a few choice curse words. The surprised glance between Hart and Swanson didn't escape her. She rarely swore compared to those two. It was their response to pretty much everything, but it wasn't her usual way of dealing with anything. Having a kid forced her to say more family-friendly things like sugar or gosh. But Bell Woods riled her. That place could disappear into a vortex for all she cared. It was right across the road from her mum's house and they used to go for walks there as kids. So she had *some* happy memories.

But it was also the same place a man chased her and Dylan in a ripped hospital gown, and it was the same place Swanson and Hart found the body of her childhood friend this past summer. Now an ache tugged at her heart whenever she drove to her mum's. Which was often, thanks to her helping with childcare for Joshua while she worked three days a week. Or every day of the week, depending on what was happening.

"And why do you think Bailey can help?" she asked Swanson.

"That's what I said to him!" Hart called from the other side of the kitchen. She noisily placed two cups on the side and opened the fridge looking for milk. "Bailey's been no help since his mental breakdown."

"He might talk to Summer," Swanson snapped at her over his shoulder. He drained his can of pop and looked pointedly at Summer. She'd never known anyone who could drain fizzy pop so quickly. "You are special to him. You're the only one he would talk to before. He doesn't trust the police; he was told to hide from us his whole life. You're the only one of us he trusted."

"He doesn't trust me anymore, though. I can try if you really want me to, but I'm not sure there's any point. I went to visit him last month and got nothing out of him. Nada. I'm not exaggerating when I say he didn't even *look* at me, never mind speak to me. Is Bell Woods the only possible connection to him?"

"So far," Swanson replied. "But I don't think it's too much of a stretch that he told someone about those bodies and that person is now using the woods too."

"Why don't we find out more about this woman first? We can check out who she was and whether she had any enemies. We do all the usual background stuff and then we can decide if there's any point trying to talk to Bailey," Hart suggested before taking her first sip of coffee and closing her eyes in delight.

"Yes. That makes sense to me." Summer nodded her agreement.

"Two against one, Swanson," Hart said. She winked across to Summer with a grin.

Swanson's eyes narrowed in annoyance. "Fine. But you're both going to be feeling silly if my hunch is correct. They usually are."

Hart shrugged and picked up her two cups of coffee. "And on that note, I'm going to do some digging of my own. I'll see you two lovebirds soon."

"Who's the other cup of coffee for, Robin?" Swanson called as she walked past him. Hart scowled even more at him using her nickname. She didn't like being the sidekick.

Summer tried to hide her grin. They both knew it was for Jane Murray, but Hart would never admit it. No affairs stayed secret in the station for long and after Charlie Marsh's death, neither seemed too bothered about the world knowing anymore. It didn't stop Murray from watching Swanson and Summer closely, though. *Hypocrite.*

"Shut up, Krypto." Hart stormed out of the kitchen, followed by Swanson's laughter.

"You two are something else," Summer said as she slouched into a chair across from him. It was almost time to go home, and the tiredness was kicking in.

"We're like an old married couple, according to Trent. Is that what you and I will be like in another few years, do you reckon? Sniping at each other over who has to get some milk or do the dishes."

"Not if that's your way of proposing," she replied in a mock offended tone, and he laughed softly.

"Let's focus on the moving in together first, eh?" he replied. "There's only two days left until you and Joshua are stuck with me full time. There's still time to change your mind."

She reached out and wrapped her hand around his imposing fist. His skin was rough but warm and familiar, and excitement bubbled in her stomach at the thought of being with him every day.

"That's the third time you've said that this week. I will not change my mind. You're stuck with me."

"That's what you think. I might change *my* mind if you and Hart keep ganging up on me like you just did there."

"No. You won't," Summer replied confidently and removed her hand from his. "You'll just ignore us and speak to Billy Bailey, regardless."

"I *was* thinking of trying to get Murray on my side. The boss always gets her way, so she'd count as two people. That would be three against two, then."

"Nice logic. You'll need to bring her something stronger than coffee to bribe her, then," Summer replied.

"True. I need to go." He stretched as he stood up. "Why are you here on a Saturday, anyway?"

"I'm only here for half an hour or so. I have a report to finish on that public indecency charge. I'll be gone by five o'clock."

"Ah. Is that the report on the man who ran through the shopping centre in town naked?"

She nodded. "That's the one."

"Trent had to go and catch him with Rob Smith." He snorted. "Was it because of beer or mental illness, do you think?"

"It was drugs."

"Fair enough. I should have guessed. I'll ring you later, then." He stepped around the table and quickly kissed her cheek before leaving. "Love you."

She smiled to herself as he walked away. The past couple of months had been great between them. Losing a colleague seemed to make Swanson realise life was for living. And now they were moving into his cosy Ockbrook cottage as a proper family. Joshua was on board with it and super excited about the cottage. It had a lot more space for him than her flat did currently. It was perfect. *But when did anything perfect stay that way?*

She pushed away the doubts and stood. It was totally normal to worry, especially as a mother. But she was certain all the way to her bones that Swanson was the right man for both her and for Joshua, and nothing was going to ruin that if she could help it.

4

Swanson

Swanson entered the pokey storage room along the corridor from the kitchen. Someone had left an old desk in it after a big grant allowed the station to get a makeover a couple of years ago. After they'd received a grant, the powers that be made the main row of offices open plan for *collaborative* working, much to Swanson's distaste. So he'd turned the cupboard into his own version of a more private office.

There were so many better things to spend money on than some hot desk nightmare. It surprised him that Murray hadn't moved him out of the cupboard yet, but dating Hart preoccupied her lately, as had the threat of losing her job after Marsh's death.

They'd kept Marsh's real identity hidden from the public so far. Hart had initially even refused to tell him most of it. She still felt she needed to protect Marsh. But it played on her mind until she was severely drunk one night and most of the real story came out. It was the story of an innocent foster kid driven to murder purely to survive the terrible hand life dealt her. And who then joined the police to make amends.

He changed from his jeans and t-shirt into the spare black suit in the corner of the office, and sat down in the old swivel chair behind the desk. He fiddled with the height to get it right again. It used to stay in the same position every time, much to his delight. But lately it had always bloody moved, and he had to fix it daily. It was probably time to steal a new one. Unless Hart was sneaking in and doing it on purpose to annoy him, which he wouldn't put past her.

He forced his mind back to the fresh case. There might have been nothing but location connecting it to Billy Bailey, but the hunch was so strong that it was impossible to ignore. And what harm could a few questions have? He'd either talk or he wouldn't. And it had been a good month or so since Summer last tried. A lot could happen in a month.

A knock at his door interrupted him before he could pick up the phone to call Bailey's hospital. He stared at the closed door. Who was so respectful they'd actually knock on his door? He couldn't think of one person. It certainly wasn't Summer or Hart, and Murray never came in. She preferred to pretend it didn't exist.

"Come in," he called cautiously.

As the door creaked open, he recognised PC Lisa Trent. She grinned briefly, showing off a full set of extra-white teeth. Or maybe they just looked so white against her tanned skin and black hair. She scraped her hair back into a bun so tight that it looked painful.

"Afternoon," she stated in her usual business-like voice. "Are you looking into this new body from Bell Woods with Hart?"

"Yes," he replied shortly.

"Good. I want to get involved. Any leads?" Trent was always straight to the point. She seemed to enjoy conversing with people as much as he did—so not very much.

It almost made him laugh now that he'd once thought Trent and Hart were having a *thing*. It turned out Hart's thing was for Marsh, until she walked in on a deep conversation between Trent and Marsh. In usual Hart style, she'd lost her temper before asking questions and split with Marsh. It turned out Lisa Trent had just figured out something was off about Marsh.

"No. We're still waiting on some reports. Although I wondered if it was connected to Billy Bailey with it being in Bell Woods."

"Hmm. He's locked up still, though, right? And the body is fresh?"

"Yes." He was getting really sick of people saying that. "It's about a day old, according to the guy on site."

"Okay. Thanks for the update, Swanson. Let me know how I can help when you have more information." She nodded curtly as she turned away and closed the door behind her.

He sat back in the wobbly chair to consider the next steps of the case. The reports needed to be completed before he could add any weight to his thought process, but he couldn't shake Billy Bailey from his mind. Even without the evidential reports, the hunch was growing stronger the more he considered it.

Screw it.

Murray might be on his side about Bailey. Asking her was worth a shot. He left the calm quiet of his own space and made his way to the rowdy open office at the end of the corridor. Police officers, both plain clothed and uniformed, sat huddled around on lines of desks discussing cases and passing on information. The incessant chatter coming from each group made him want to wear earplugs. How anyone could work in this mess was really unbelievable.

Murray's office was at the far end, because of course she'd ensured she still had her own, much quieter space. There would be no collaboration from her anytime soon. He rapped his knuckles on the door. It was more aggressive than he meant to and made a few officers behind him turn in surprise.

"No," Murray yelled, right before a loud crash.

Adrenaline flooded his body. His mind was already riled up from the dead body, and he acted on instinct. He pushed open the door so hard that the lock bolt snapped on the other side.

"Are you okay?" he yelled.

But when he saw what was happening, he immediately closed the door again. His face flushed red hot as his brain processed what he'd witnessed. There was smashed glass on the floor, and next to the desk were Hart and Murray . . . *together*. Murray did collaborate after all.

Shit. Shit. Shit.

His career was over. Murray would never forgive him for bursting in on them. *Would Hart? Probably not.* They were generally as angry as each other. No wonder they ended up getting together. It wasn't his fault the cheap lock bolt broke from a small shove. He'd barely touched the damn thing.

"Er." He looked at the door and considered what to say. His nose was almost touching the wood and he could feel the nosy glares of staff behind him wondering what had happened. There was silence from inside her office. "I'm going to see Billy Bailey in the hospital. I think he might have something to do with the body in Bell W—"

"Yes, fine! Just go, Swanson," Murray yelled back.

The annoyance in her voice was clear. He was a dead man

once she regained her sensibilities. And Hart would probably do worse to him. His cheeks burned as he dashed away, convinced he would never return. But before making his escape, Lisa Trent blocked his path for another chat.

"Hi, Swanson. I've been looking for you." She tilted her head. "Are you okay? Your face is a bit . . . pink. And you're sweating."

"Yes, I'm fine," he blurted. "How can I help?"

"This came in." She handed him a folded up piece of plain, white paper.

He took it from her and opened it up quickly. In between the creases was a name that he read out loud.

"Dotty Foster." The name was not familiar at all. "Who is she?"

"Dotty Foster is someone who can tell us all about the now *identified* body in Bell Woods. Or so we hope, anyway." Trent shrugged.

"So we have a name for the body already?" he asked.

He risked a glance behind his shoulder to look at Murray's office. No one had come out yet. They probably didn't know the body had been identified. There was no way he was going in to tell them. He needed to go away before her or Hart came out to bury him.

"We think so. It looks like she was called Mandy Harris," Trent continued, oblivious to his current plight. "There was a photo ID in her pocket, which was very handy. It was also complete with an address. But the address isn't registered to Mandy Harris, it's registered to someone called Dotty Foster. Which is the same name noted as the next of kin on her medical records."

"That was quick," Swanson observed.

"Yep. The address is written on there too. One of the other

officers was going to speak to her, but I thought you and Hart might want to check it out first with it being Bell Woods and your hunch on Billy Bailey."

"Yes. Sure. 'Course. Thanks for bringing it to us, Trent. Hart's busy at the minute, but I will go. Can you tell Murray what you've just told me, please? She's in her office. Make sure you knock, she's in a bad mood." He folded the paper and shoved it in his pocket. He pointed behind Trent. "I just have to do something urgently in that direction before I visit Dotty Foster. Bye."

He pushed open the door behind Trent and rushed away to the safety of the corridor. No way did he want to be in that space when Hart eventually appeared.

"Let me know how you get on," Trent called after him as the door closed softly in between them.

He didn't answer her or return to his office as he'd planned. Instead, he stormed towards the rear exit of the station and out into the staff car park. As soon as he opened the door, the freezing air slapped him in the face. He breathed it in deeply as he stood at the top of the short set of concrete steps that led to the car park. He finally felt the blushing fade and the beads of sweat on his forehead dry up.

He pulled himself together and jogged down the steps. He'd parked his car in its usual safe spot — across the car park at the end of the far row. Fewer people parked back there because they were too lazy to walk an extra hundred or two feet. Plus, the end space meant less chance of some idiot opening their car door into his. The damn spaces were so small compared to the size of modern cars.

The wintry afternoon light had dimmed so quickly that his car was barely visible compared to when he'd parked up. It was now pitch black. The only light was courtesy of the street lamps dotted around the station grounds. Summer hated the cold, dark nights, but they suited him just fine. Other than the additional Christmas traffic December brought to the city.

He breathed another sigh of relief once he was safely in the driver's seat and quickly dragged the seatbelt across his broad chest to click it into place. There was something about getting into the car that just felt soothing.

He forced his mind clear of Hart and Murray and that entire nightmare. He would never think of it again. Not even in passing. He pulled his focus to check out Dotty Foster's address. At nearly 5 p.m. it was too late in the day to visit Bailey; the psychiatric hospital probably wouldn't let anyone in past their usual visiting hours. But he hoped Dotty could be a great help.

It was interesting to see that Dotty Foster, and possibly Mandy Harris, lived on 22 Feanor Road. Because that was the main road that ran alongside Bell Woods, with houses in parallel to the same section of the woods that someone had dragged Mandy's body to and then abandoned. The garden of 22 Feanor Road likely backed straight onto the woods.

Though his stomach was empty, and he needed a snack break before he saw Dotty Foster. He threw a quick text to ask Aunt Barb to meet him at Darley Abbey cafe. He only had to wait a minute before she replied to confirm she'd be there soon. He was lucky she wasn't out at some dramatic show or drinking gin with a neighbour on a Saturday evening. She had a better social life than most young people.

A bang made him snap his neck up. The back door of the station had slammed shut. Hart stood at the top of the steps, and she was looking straight at him. The wall lights from each side of the door bathed her in an eerie golden glow. His palms were sticky with sweat.

She surely couldn't actually see him in this darkness, but she knew damn well where his car would be. That's the problem with having a routine—everyone knows it. He averted his gaze in case she could somehow see him and flicked on the engine. She didn't move as he sped out of the car park, and he pretended not to look at her. But from his rearview mirror he could see her silhouette standing there, arms crossed, and her head followed him all the way until he was out of view.

He followed the main road round to Darley Abbey Park. It would usually take only a few minutes to drive there, but thanks to the Christmas rush it took double the usual time. Aunt Barb lived round the corner from the park, and she was waiting at their usual spot when he entered. Though she was so well wrapped up in a pink woolly hat and scarf that he didn't realise it was her at first.

She sat on a small wooden bench at the top of the hill that led to the park, but stood when she saw him coming. Her flowery dress fluttered around her black ankle boots, and her elegant red coat was almost down to her knees.

"There you are, Alex." She greeted him in her usual clipped accent and put her arms out to hug him, one of few people who could get away with such close contact unscathed.

"Hi, Barb." He hugged her with one arm, the other firmly in his pocket.

He breathed in the familiar woody scent of her most prized perfume as she linked her arm in his. The same one she insisted he buy for her birthday each year. He couldn't help but notice she felt a bit more frail than normal. It wasn't really a surprise now that she was in her seventies, but she still looked so elegant all the time it was easy to forget her age. He forgot about the

Hart mishap as they walked arm in arm down the trail to reach their favourite cafe.

"We're a bit late today, darling. It's almost closing time," Barb mused as they reached the courtyard of the little building.

"Shall we just have a drink?"

"Absolutely not," she replied, horrified, and let go of his arm to turn to him. "You're wasting away, Alex. Let's at least get a sausage roll each."

He laughed hard. Aunt Barb was the only person in the world who would say he was wasting away. He unlinked his arm from hers and went to the window of the cafe. A young girl was serving, and he ordered tea for Barb and two large sausage rolls. Barb ate a lot for someone who'd always been so slim.

His mum was the same. Or she had been slim the last time he'd seen her, which was some time ago. The skinny gene had certainly missed him out, though he didn't mind being broad. They sat down on a pair of cold metal chairs left out on the patio.

"Why did you want to meet so last minute, dear?" she asked as she removed the sausage roll from its paper bag. Steam floated from the pastry as she took her first bite. He could feel his cheeks heating again as the memory came back to him.

"No reason. I just wanted to eat. Plus, we didn't get to meet last week when I was helping Summer pack up her flat."

"Ah, the elusive Summer. We could do with a bit of her in this weather. When will I get to meet this lovely lady, then?" she asked, her blue eyes twinkling.

He thought for a minute as he chewed on his own sausage roll, swallowing the hot pastry before answering. "I'll have to check with Summer but how does next Sunday sound? When we've settled in a bit and got stuff unpacked."

"That sounds perfect. Make sure she brings that gorgeous little boy. I have a present for him all ready. Now, are you going to tell me what's wrong?" She smiled knowingly at him as she took another bite.

"Nothing's wrong, Aunt Barb. Promise." He hesitated, knowing she wouldn't drop it unless he told her something. And he was rubbish at lying to her. "It was just a slightly embarrassing situation at work that I wish hadn't happened."

"Those are the best ones. You'll laugh about it soon. How about we have some whiskey at mine? That'll loosen your tongue. I've got that expensive stuff you like."

He grinned. "I need to do an interview now. There was a body found in the woods in Ilkeston today."

"Ah, of course. Your job is important. We can do it another time."

He took her empty paper bag and scrunched it up with his own for the bin.

"We'll do it on Sunday. Summer doesn't drink when she has Joshua, so she won't mind driving."

"Sounds perfect." She beamed up at him and he put out his arm for her to grab on to as she got up. "You make sure you tell those bosses of yours you've got plans, won't you?"

"I will," he replied as they sauntered back to the car park. "Come on, I may as well drop you off at home on my way to Ilkeston. It's freezing."

It only took a minute to drive around the corner and drop Barb off outside her ridiculously enormous house. He watched as she walked up to the front door, waiting until she was safely inside before he drove off.

Then he turned right to head towards the A52 to Ilkeston. It was about twenty-five minutes away with minimal traffic on the dual carriageway. That gave him time to forget all about what happened and get focussed on the case. Hart could wait until tomorrow. Where they would have the time and space to think about it and then pretend it never happened like good friends did.

5

Swanson

Again the drive back to Ilkeston took much longer than usual thanks to the hundreds of Christmas shoppers driving home on the A52. It was the same every year in the city on the run up to the big day, but for once Swanson didn't mind. He turned up the heat and leaned back in the driver's seat as he queued in the left lane. It allowed him time to clear his mind following what he'd witnessed, and he used the time to think about Mandy Harris and focus on what to say to Dotty Foster.

He wondered how she'd react to being informed about the death of Mandy Harris. He'd experienced all sorts of reactions from violence to devastation. It was hard to gauge without knowing how they knew each other, and he really needed to know how they were related before he presented the news. As her next of kin, they must have been close. Possibly a couple. He eventually passed the entrance to Bell Woods on Feanor Road. It was still taped off with a police car blocking the entrance. They may have paused the search for evidence until the light returned in the morning. Woodland was hard enough to search without daylight, and the cold weather was at least dry for a change.

He continued past the entrance and pulled up outside number 22. The houses he'd passed on the road were a mismatch of smaller semi's, huge detached houses, and even bungalows. But it surprised him to see how nice number 22 was compared to the average, red brick semi's that were most common along the road.

It was easily the biggest he'd noticed on the long road. A sturdy-looking fence and a black double gate framed the land, and someone had recently paid a lot of money for it to be rendered in fresh white on every surface. The matte grey door and matching window sills gave it a much more modern look than the plain properties that surrounded it. It had certainly cost someone a pretty penny within the last year. Though it wasn't necessarily nicer in Swanson's opinion.

He pushed open the heavy gate and stepped cautiously along the curved path that led to the front door. He half expected a security guard to jump out from nowhere and tell him to go away. Neatly trimmed grass surrounded the path, and he briefly wondered how they'd got it looking so good considering the time of year. It was a stark contrast to his own lawn which was a mixture of dead grass and overgrown weeds.

He approached the panelled door and knocked loudly, ignoring the doorbell. Most of them didn't work. Though this one probably did seeing as someone had put so much work into how the house looked. He noted that there were no Christmas decorations anywhere yet. Or at least any that were visible from the outside. Not too unusual considering it was only the second of December. Swanson wouldn't have any himself if it wasn't for Joshua excitedly bringing him a small pre-lit tree round last week. Summer had already forewarned him that it would get much worse after they moved in.

He noticed some movement behind the glass panel of the door, and a second later it flew open. A slim woman with a shiny, blonde bob stood before him. Black square glasses framed her pale face. She was easily in her sixties judging from her wrinkled face, but dressed much younger in skin-tight jeans and a camel-coloured cashmere top. A book was in her hand, though he couldn't see the title. She looked him up and down, clearly annoyed he'd had the gall to interrupt her reading time.

"Can I help you?" she asked in a posh accent not unlike Aunt Barb's.

"I hope so. I'm Detective Inspector Alex Swanson." He flashed his ID badge. "Can I come in, please?"

"What is it about?" she asked. She crossed her arms, still blocking the doorway and showing no signs of moving.

"It's about someone called Mandy Harris. I believe she may be a friend of yours?" He observed her reaction carefully. Her expression softened and her arms fell to her side.

"Mandy? She's my sister. Is she okay?"

A knot of guilt about being the one to tell her pulled at his stomach. Hart was much better at this stuff. He instantly regretted not waiting for her.

"It really would be better to talk inside. I'm afraid I have some bad news," he replied gently.

Her shoulders sagged, and she stood aside to let him step onto the grey oak flooring of a large hallway. Or at least it was large compared to his cramped cottage. A black carpet covered the stairs straight ahead, and the walls were lined with glittery wallpaper covered in tropical-looking birds. It was all very strange. Hopefully, Summer won't want anything like that. A living room was off to the left, and he followed Dotty inside it once she'd closed the front door. His eye was drawn to a thick oak coffee table in the middle of the room, which was shaped like a map of the UK.

"Please sit." She pointed at a sleek white sofa.

Thick blue cushions covered so much of it, he wasn't sure where to actually sit. He took extra care not to knock any of the expensive knickknacks dotted around as he took a seat. Dotty placed her book on the table and sat down on the far end of the sofa. She bit her bottom lip nervously. He clenched his jaw and prepared himself to deliver the news, knowing that to Dotty, his face would forever be associated with the death of her sister.

"I'm so sorry to tell you this, Dotty. We found a body in Bell Woods this morning. The ID seems to confirm it is Mandy. It also had this address on it, hence why I'm here."

Though she didn't react or burst into tears, the pain was written all over Dotty's face. His heart went out to her. Hart would know what to say. She continued in a smaller voice.

"Are you sure it's her?" she asked. "I only saw her yesterday."

"The picture on the ID matched the body," Swanson repeated. He stayed quiet to give her time to process what he'd said. She stared at the floor and sniffed back a tear.

"Would you like me to get you a tissue? Or call somebody?"

She shook her head. "You said you found her in the woods. What happened to her? Did she fall? She's very clumsy."

"We're unsure what happened to her at the minute, but it looks like a third party may have been involved." He avoided using the word murdered. "Some injuries on her body suggest she was attacked. I was hoping you could help us piece it together and catch the person responsible for hurting her."

"Someone hurt her?" Dotty swallowed hard and looked back up at him.

"Possibly. Has she recently fallen out with anyone? A partner, perhaps?"

"Not that I can think of." She shook her head sadly.

"Is this her main residence?"

"Yes. We share the bills here together."

"Where did you think she was last night?"

"Sorry?" Her head snapped up to face him.

"You mentioned you hadn't seen her since yesterday. Is that unusual? I just wondered why no one had reported her missing."

She stood up from the sofa, and Swanson took her lead and got to his feet. "I need you to go."

She fiddled with the edge of her top and sniffed again before walking over to the front door. Swanson followed her through the hallway. He turned to her once they reached the door.

"I completely understand you will need time to process this, Dotty. But we really need your help. Mandy needs you. If you can please call us as soon as you're ready to talk."

"Yes, of course." She nodded her head, and he handed her a business card as he exited the house.

"Are you going to be okay? Shall I call anyone for you?" he asked again.

"Mandy is the only person I would usually call when something happens," she said sadly. "Well, thank you for your time."

With that she closed the door in his face. Charming. But everyone dealt with such news differently. He couldn't say he wouldn't react the same way if a stranger turned up to him to discuss the death of a family member. It wasn't personal.

He got back in the car to head to Ockbrook and the wonky cottage he called home. It was five miles east of the police station, but the drive was about fifteen minutes from Ilkeston; enough time to call Summer to see if she'd made it back to her flat yet with Joshua. She answered on the second ring, and her voice filled his car through the speaker.

"Hey, sorry, hold on one sec. Joshua! Your dinner is getting cold," she yelled.

He winced. As much as he loved her and Joshua, their presence in his peaceful cottage was going to take a lot of getting used to.

"Sorry about that. Everything okay?" she asked breathlessly.

"Sure," Swanson said. "I'm just heading home and wanted to check on you guys."

"Aw. We're fine. Not long now until we'll be a part of your home and we'll be there waiting for you when you have to work late." She sounded so happy, and he couldn't help but grin.

"I can't wait," he replied, despite the gnawing sensation in the back of his brain that something was about to go wrong.

"You don't sound so sure!" She laughed, but there was a definite edge of concern in her tone.

"I'm sure," he reassured her. "Of course I am."

"Okay. If you say so. I need to eat dinner, but I'll call later. Let me know if you want to pop round."

"Will do."

She hung up, and he drove the rest of the way listening to indie rock music DJ Scott Flood. He wondered if Summer ever listened to Scott Flood. He didn't even know if she liked indie rock music. Maybe they were moving too fast if he didn't even know the answer to such a simple question.

Or he could just ask her—tonight. It felt urgent somehow that he knew the answer.

The crunch of gravel under the heavy tyres overtook the music as he arrived in the cottage's driveway. He drove on sideways and took up most of the land—not that there was loads of room in the first place. But that would have to stop soon so Summer could park her BMW on it alongside.

The cottage was behind a Moravian Church, one of very few Moravian settlements in the UK. It was one he knew well, thanks to his stepdad. Not that he was around anymore. His mother finally left him last year, and she had lived alone ever since.

She hadn't met Summer and Joshua yet, and probably wouldn't until closer to Christmas. His relationship with Aunt Barb was closer to mother and son than his own mum, thanks to the same stepdad. That would be an interesting visit. Summer would get to see their messed up family dynamic for real.

There was no hallway in the cottage like at Dotty Foster's. The front door opened straight up into the living room. The space was off balance, thanks to the far right wall, which wasn't quite straight; it made the whole cottage tilt.

It was still the best room in the building. The sofa was ridiculously comfortable but ancient, and a freebie as the previous owners left it. His TV, console, and mini fridge were all in the one room. Not that he had much time to appreciate the TV or gaming. The kitchen was straight behind it, and there was even a small toilet under the stairs. He barely needed the upstairs - another thing that would change with two extra people.

Something else was different in the cottage that night. He

felt it as soon as he closed the front door and turned the key in the lock. The hair on the back of his neck creeped up. He shrugged it off and turned around. The living room looked just as it always did. Other than the thick atmosphere that made his skin tingle as if he wasn't the only one in the room.

His phone beeped, but he ignored it and stood still. He surveyed the room in silence, waiting for a noise or clue of what was giving him such an awful feeling. But there was nothing. No cries or tricks from Joshua. No laughter or shouts from Summer.

Unless that was the issue. It was possible he couldn't wait for this ancient little cottage to finally be a proper home with noise, and laughter, and cars squished on to the driveway side by side every night. Maybe the weird dread in the pit of his stomach was actually excitement, and the heavy atmosphere that surrounded him was loneliness exacerbated by the silence that he was no longer used to. It could have been Summer messaging his phone. He pulled it from his pocket to check, almost overcome with a need to hear her voice. But the text wasn't from Summer. It was from AnonTxTNow.

You're getting closer, Alex Swanson. But you need to stay away from Billy Bailey.

He stared at the message, unable to make sense of it. He hit Reply, knowing he probably shouldn't.

Who is this? Is that a helpful hint or a threat?

He kicked off his shoes as he waited for a reply and double-checked he'd locked the front door. He flicked off the living room light and stuck his head through the curtains to check if anyone was out on the front, but it was empty from what little he could see in the dark.

If you want me to stay away from your family, you need to stay away from Billy Bailey.

6

Summer

Summer pushed down the power button on the dishwasher and sat at the table with a small glass of white wine. The whooshing of the machine filled the kitchen as if the old appliance was struggling and about to retire any minute. Swanson's earlier call had thrown her off balance, and she sighed heavily. There was no dishwasher at the cottage, and the kitchen was small. She'd have to fit one in somewhere. Cooking was fine, but doing the dishes? *Ugh.*

Well, she would fit one in *if* Swanson still wanted them to move in with him. He hadn't sounded too sure over the phone. The pauses, and his tone, did not fill her with confidence that he was as excited about it as when he asked her to move in.

He might be getting cold feet. Hell, maybe it was all in her head and *she* was getting cold feet. This flat had been home for so long that it would be hard to leave. It was the only home Joshua could remember, other than going to stay at his dad's house on the weekends. If they had to leave the flat for something that didn't end up working out then that would suck tenfold. The guilt would be unbearable.

She had always been grateful that at least he was too young to remember her and his dad breaking up. He didn't seem massively affected by it, and they all got along okay. His stepmum was lovely, and he had a little sister to argue with. He heard no one bad-mouthing anyone else. It was perfect as far as blended families went.

But at eight-years-old Joshua was big enough to remember everything now. If it didn't work out with Swanson, it could have an actual effect on him. She shuddered at the thought.

There was no way she was putting him through that crap more than once. It either worked out with Swanson or no one at all until Joshua was eighteen years old. Or twenty-one. Or thirty.

"Mummy!" Joshua sprinted into the kitchen at speed. Why were kids always rushing when they had nowhere to be? It didn't happen on school mornings.

"Yes, babe?" she asked.

He threw himself across the kitchen and ran into her arms. She laughed and kissed the top of his head.

"Slow down! You just ate your dinner and it will come back up."

"I'm too excited!" He beamed as he looked up at her through the gap in her arms.

"About what?" she asked.

"The cottage! It's an entire house just for us three." He pulled away from her grasp and waved his arms about in a funny dance.

"Aw. Are you excited about all three of us living together?" she asked for the millionth time, desperate to be sure she was doing the right thing.

"I can't wait, Mummy. It's going to be great. We can play

games together every day! And play football and watch films."
He fist pumped the air and ran off again towards the living room
yelling. "I'm too excited to stand, I'm going to sit down."

"I'm running you a bath now. You've got ten minutes," she
called after him, wistfully wishing for some of his energy.

"I can't hear you, Mummy," he yelled back with a giggle.
"That means no bath!"

She rolled her eyes. He was getting cheekier every day. But
it warmed her heart to see how excited he was about moving
into the cottage. It would be good for him to have someone else
around.

Another sibling would be even better.

She couldn't help a smile thinking of the look of panic
Swanson would give her if she suggested a baby so soon.
Though she was pretty sure a woman's fertility lessened after
thirty-something. She grabbed her phone from the table to
look it up, but as soon as she picked it up it rang. As if he'd read
her mind, Swanson was calling again. Which was weird for him.
He was far more of a text kind of guy, two calls in one evening
was very unusual.

"Hey, Summer. Are you both okay?" His words were rushed
and garbled, and immediately caused a surge of worry.

"Hey, are *you* okay?" she asked tentatively.

"Yes, I'm fine," he replied quickly. "But are you two okay?"

"Yes. We're fine too. Why wouldn't we be?" She rubbed her
stomach to calm the sudden nausea.

He ignored her question. "Are you at home?"

"Yes, babe. What's going on?" she asked again. Her worry
was fast turning into annoyance. He was always so shady.

"Did anything strange happen today?"

"Oh my god, Swanson!" she snapped. She pushed herself

up from the dining room chair and paced the kitchen floor. "Please, just tell me what's going on. You're acting really weird."

"There's nothing going on!" he snapped back. "I got home recently and instantly had a weird feeling about something. I wanted to check everything was fine. That's all."

"Hmm." She paused her pacing and leaned on the kitchen counter instead.

No words came to her. So much for being a psychologist. Swanson was such a stoic, big bear of a man who seemed scared of nothing. It was so unlike him to be this nervy.

"Are *you* sure you're okay?" she asked again.

"Yes. As long as you stay safe then I will be fine. Just keep your door locked. I'm sure it's nothing." He sounded distracted, as if he was searching for something.

"Well, you will be able to keep us both safe soon," she replied. A smile played on her lips as she waited for his reply, but there was silence at the other end. "Swanson?"

"Yes. Of course. I need to get going, but promise me you'll keep that door locked."

He was definitely paying attention to something else.

"I promise."

Then the line went dead. Great. That was calm and reassuring. It was just what she needed right before giving up her and Joshua's home and committing to another man that might break her heart. She cursed and went to run the bath for Joshua, wondering if it was too late to renew the rental agreement on the flat. There was no harm in knowing her options.

She walked into the corridor to head to the bathroom door, but her feet turned the other way to double check she'd locked the front door. She pulled on the handle, which didn't budge, and made sure the chain was across the door. Damn Swanson and his paranoia. But she shuddered as she walked away with the feeling that eyes were watching her from somewhere, and it wasn't a friendly glare.

7

Swanson

S wanson groaned as the radio alarm on his phone blared an annoying pop tune across the living room. He felt around for the device to shut it off before realising it was on the other side of the room somewhere. Even with the incessant beat cutting into his brain it took a minute to open his tired eyes. He stretched out his sore body.

It occurred to him that this was probably one of the last nights falling asleep alone on the sofa. Summer would expect to share a bed like they did when she slept over. That would be a good thing, if not least for his back. His body was getting too old for this crap.

He whipped the thin blanket off his bare chest and forced his aching limbs into a sitting position. The evening before played on his mind as he remembered what happened. The text had made him too antsy to go to bed, and he'd fallen asleep on the sofa before getting undressed. Though in the night he'd thrown off his T-shirt and slept only in grey joggers. A pint of water sat on the wooden floor next to him, and he downed it before getting up to turn the damn alarm off.

He breathed in and enjoyed the silence. Too bad he couldn't just stay in the cottage for the day in peace. He double-checked the phone for any more anonymous messages or anything from Hart or Summer.

Nothing.

It crossed his mind how amazing life would be if yesterday was all a dream. There would be no dead bodies, no creepy messages, and no walking in on Hart and Murray. The last thought made him shudder enough to get moving, and he ran upstairs to take a shower.

The five-minute shower helped to clear his mind, and he was feeling better by the time he was dry with freshly cleaned teeth. From the old wardrobe in the bedroom he pulled out a dark suit; the lamp wasn't bright enough in the bedroom to tell whether it was black or navy, and the big light bulb had gone weeks ago. He made a mental note to change it before Summer arrived and pulled out a collared blue shirt and a dark tie. The tie was definitely some sort of dark blue.

He skipped breakfast for another glass of water and shoved his feet into black shoes that used to look smart but were now scuffed along each outside edge. Hart had threatened to buy him some new ones for Christmas. He hoped she would. It would save him a shopping trip.

After an hour of fighting through Christmas traffic, he was back at the station in his pokey office. Summer wasn't usually in on a Sunday, nor were he or Hart as a general rule. But when there was something as serious as a murder, their hours changed to all day every day until the risk to the public was diminished.

So Hart was probably around somewhere. He'd considered going to find her to tell her about the anonymous message but thought better of it. Hart was already snappy when nothing was wrong, but she was like a mother bear protecting its young when embarrassed about something. She was probably gunning for his head on a stick.

But his office door flew open within ten minutes of sitting at his desk, and Hart stormed in with slightly pink cheeks and a stout expression. His whole body stiffened in his chair.

"Morning, Swanson," she said with an awkward nod.

"Morning," he replied, sounding more nervous than her.

"Dotty Foster called regarding Mandy Harris. She said you went to see her yesterday. She wants to talk to a female officer, so I'm going to chat with her." Hart's tone was business-like and to the point. "I'll go alone."

"Fair enough. I haven't done a report yet, but she didn't give me much yesterday. All I really found out was that Mandy is her sister. Or *was*. And that one or both of them had money, and they lived in that house together. Someone has recently done it up to the nines. She hadn't seen Mandy since Friday, but didn't explain why she hadn't called her in as missing if you can find that out. Maybe she went to stay with a friend or partner. Also, I need to see Billy Bailey today."

"I thought we agreed going to speak to him was a waste of time? It's not like he'll talk to anyone. He doesn't even say good morning."

"No. *You* said it would be a waste of time, but I didn't agree. Plus, I got two strange text messages last night from an anonymous user that mentioned him. Look here."

He brought up the messages on his phone and held it up to show Hart the screen. Despite their initial weird vibe, she stepped over to his desk and perched on the edge as she would usually. Her eyes widened as she read the messages, and she

47

grabbed the phone from his hand to look more closely.

"Swanson! Why didn't you tell me about these messages yesterday?" she asked. "You should have called me when you received them."

He hesitated, not wanting to bring up what happened and how awkward it had made him feel. "I don't know. I guess I fell asleep."

"Why are you like this?" She tutted and dropped his phone back onto the desk. Back to business as usual it was then. "You need to report that to Murray and get someone on it to find out who's behind the anonymous number."

"I will. I've only just got in—"

"And what do they mean to stay *away* from your family? You don't have anyone, really."

"Thanks for that, Hart."

"Oh, sorry. I meant to think that in my head. You know what I mean, though. Summer isn't family yet is she? How would this person know she's planning on moving in with Joshua? And then you barely see your mum except for birthdays."

"Yes, again. Thanks for that, Hart. You always make me feel great."

She snapped her mouth shut and looked at him. "I am sorry. I'm actually trying to make you feel better rather than worse."

"Please explain to me how that is supposed to make me feel better," he said wearily.

"The text is an empty threat. It sounds to me like they don't know you at all and you have nothing to worry about. Otherwise they would be more specific. Don't you think so?"

He sat down again and let her words sink in. She made sense in fairness.

"Harsh but true." He nodded.

"You don't need a big family. You have Summer, me, and your Aunt Barb. I love her. She's better than any mother could be. Definitely better than mine."

He grinned. "Yeah, Barb's all right. I'm going to see Bailey today, anyway. You are probably right, but I think it's worth a shot. Just in case he has an epiphany and decides to tell me everything."

"Perfect. Go and see him now and we'll meet back for lunch to swap notes." She turned and waltzed off towards the door.

"Yes, sir," he muttered sarcastically.

"Piss off, Swanson. See you here at lunch."

Thankful that the awkwardness had dissipated so quickly between them, he grabbed his phone and called the hospital to let them know he needed to speak to Bailey and would be there shortly. The woman he spoke to seemed about as uninterested as a human could be. It didn't surprise him. They weren't exactly nice places to visit, never mind work in. Some of the horror stories Summer had told him about how staff were treated were horrendous. And not by patients but by hospital management.

The hospital Billy Bailey lived in was actually over in Nottingham rather than Derby. Gold Bay Hospital was a secure unit that looked after adult men who were diagnosed with a range of different personality disorders. Summer had already informed him that a doctor there had diagnosed Bailey with catatonic schizophrenia because of his lack of reaction to things around him and being mute since the deaths of his sisters. She'd explained in a bit more detail but he was pretty sure that was the basic gist of her psychobabble. She got so animated when she talked about psychology that sometimes he got too invested in her movements and forgot to actually listen.

The hospital was just off the dual carriageway of the A52 not far from Nottingham's bustling city centre. He'd almost chosen to move to Nottingham when moving to the midlands years ago, but Aunt Barb had convinced him to go to Ockbrook where his mother was. Though he'd done it purely for Barb. At that time he didn't even speak to his mother.

And it may have been partly out of spite for his stepdad.

Nottingham was the largest city in the midlands, other than Birmingham, and with two universities, two hospitals, and two football clubs on top of all the shops, bars, and restaurants, it was always busy. Then there was the legend of Robin Hood and the "castle." Derby was a quiet and quaint city in comparison, which suited Swanson much better.

Despite Sunday usually being a quieter day on the roads, driving anywhere near Nottingham in December was a recipe for disaster. Even with trying to get it over and done with earlier in the day, he sat in traffic for at least half an hour trying to get around the city to the hospital. But eventually he pulled up in the small car park and carefully manoeuvred the Audi into a far corner space.

The hospital was an impressive building that the council had constructed only a decade prior. The bricks were curved so the structure was shaped like a semicircle. Unlike the last psychiatric hospital he'd visited, this was a nice place with a friendly atmosphere when he walked through the wide entrance doors. Though the walls were all blindingly white and it still smelled of medicine and sweat.

He ignored the seating area in the corner and walked straight up to the slim woman who sat behind the reception desk. It wasn't the usual, open reception area of a hospital. This reception was a separate room where the woman sat alone, protected by thick glass.

She was reading something he couldn't see on her desk, and sipped from a can of pop through a long, metal straw. Thin black hair fell over her face, and her overly thick makeup sat in the deep lines of her skin. She was definitely a smoker judging from the wrinkles. It made him want to put his own cigarettes in the bin. She didn't look up as he approached.

"Good morning," he said brightly.

The woman took a long sip of her drink before she looked up. She gave him a thin smile that seemed to take her a lot of effort.

"Good morning."

"I'm Detective Inspector Alex Swanson." He flashed his ID. "I called earlier. I'm not sure if it was you I spoke to. I'm here to speak to a patient named Billy Bailey."

"Here you go." She handed him a clipboard with a form and a pen stuck to it. "Fill this in and return it first, please. You can sit over there."

He took the clipboard but didn't move. He filled in the questions on the form right in front of her on the desk, much to her annoyance judging by the glance she provided. The form gave a list of prohibited items, which needed to go into a locker, such as lighters and pens, and asked for a signature to confirm he understood he left them at his own risk.

"This says I'm not allowed my mobile phone?" he asked the woman.

"Nope. Needs to stay down here." She handed him a key and a small black circular object. "Here's your alarm. Use it if you see anything. Don't be a hero and don't touch a patient if they kick off, because you might hurt them. Push the alarm instead. And here's the key for the locker. Number 12 is yours. Don't forget it. The key isn't labelled. Dr Riley will be here in a sec to take you through."

He muttered a few choice words under his breath when he saw the small size of the lockers. And then he had to fiddle with the key in the lock for at least a minute before it finally twisted correctly and opened up the small space. He shoved his jacket inside, along with his car key and wallet. The wallet slipped out and onto the floor twice before he jammed it inside and threw the locker door shut; he twisted the key and turned around, flustered.

A pretty blonde woman stood behind him with her arms crossed. She couldn't have been any older than late twenties, and she wore black jeans and a blue sweater. There was a lanyard swinging around her neck with a photo ID attached to the end, though he couldn't read the tiny letters from where he stood.

"DI Swanson?" She held out her hand and smiled at him expectantly.

"Yes." He stepped forward to grab her hand and shook it lightly. "Are you here to take me to Dr Riley?"

She laughed delicately, showing off perfect teeth. "No. I *am* Dr Riley. Jessica Riley. I'm one of the psychiatrists here at Goldbay Hospital. Follow me, please."

Wow. Since when did doctors start being so much younger than him? And now she must think he was sexist, when it was really more ageism. Though in his defence she wasn't wearing a white lab coat, either.

He wondered whether to explain his ageism as he followed her through the first door to the right of the reception. Was being ageist better than being sexist? Or he should just apologise.

The happy receptionist buzzed them through the first door, which led to a small square space with another door ahead. The first door locked automatically behind them. Swanson had seen these before in hospitals and prisons. There were two sets of doors with a space in between for safety reasons. But in this small space they could still see the reception through another panel of safety glass, and she rolled her chair over to that end of her room to face them once more.

"Sign in here, please," she said, pointing at a logbook in front of the glass.

Dr Riley signed back in first, noting the time she returned. Swanson signed his name again and the time in. Only then did the receptionist buzz them in through the second door.

"Sorry about her," Dr Riley said as they entered another blindingly white corridor. "She can be miserable."

"I don't know what you mean. She looked like she was full of rainbows to me," Swanson replied.

Dr Riley laughed again. She was seemingly unfazed by his earlier comments as she led him down the corridor to another airlock.

"Billy Bailey is on Rose Ward. That's our highest security ward for newer patients. We haven't moved him on yet as he still isn't communicating with me. Or anyone else for that matter. So I'm not sure if you will get anything out of him. I'd suggest a member of staff attends with you."

"Yes, please. He will need an appropriate adult with him, although it's not really an interview. It's more of an informal chat. If he talks or knows anything that can help then I might need to take him in for an interview at some point. You could stay in on the interview if you have time?"

"Sure. That's fine with me."

"Are you specifically his doctor whilst he's here?"

"Yes. I'm one of the psychiatrists for his ward. There's three of us because the patients are so challenging."

He vaguely wondered whether the other doctors were also so much younger than him. But a few minutes later they entered a small room, which was empty except for a table with four chairs angled around it. He hoped it wasn't a therapy room. It was less comfortable than the interview rooms back at the station.

"Wait here, please. I'll get Billy. It shouldn't take long." She tried to leave but hesitated halfway across the threshold and turned back to Swanson. "We have made Billy aware that you're coming, but he didn't react."

Swanson nodded, and she left, closing the door behind her. He sat in the chair furthest away and turned it to face the door. They'd at least painted this room a light blue colour rather than the harsh whiteness of the hallway. Now he was sitting, he also noticed they'd dotted pieces of amateur artwork that cited calming quotes on the wall. He read through them as he waited for Dr Riley to return.

It's okay not to be okay.

Your struggles do not define you.

You are worthy of happiness.

Cute. It didn't take long for the door to open again and Dr Riley reappeared. She pushed the door open and moved out of the way to let Billy Bailey shuffle slowly into the room.

He looked even skinnier than Swanson remembered and somehow shorter, probably thanks to how much his shoulders sagged. His hair had grown to his shoulders now, but was just as dirty. Pimples covered his face, and his presence filled the room with a greasy stench. The smell reminded him of a mechanic's garage.

"Hi, Billy," Swanson said as Bailey took a chair across from him. "I'm Detective Inspector Alex Swanson. Do you remember me from the police station?"

Billy stared at the table. His dark eyes were dead. He hadn't been the most animated person prior to his sisters' deaths, but now he didn't so much as blink. Dr Riley carefully took the seat next to him and watched him closely.

"I found Summer Thomas for you when you came to the police station looking for her because you needed help. Your brother, Andy, told you to come and see us."

Still Billy said nothing. Dr Riley glanced at Swanson sympathetically and shrugged one shoulder minutely.

"I'm not here to talk about that, though. I've actually come to ask you about another case, Billy. I'd really appreciate it if you could let me know if you've heard of a lady called Mandy Harris."

No response. Bailey didn't even look like he was breathing. An idea slowly came to Swanson. But it was risky, and he'd have to admit to breaking the rules.

Fuck it.

"I've got something to show you which might jog your memory."

He pulled out the phone he'd kept hidden in his trouser pocket. Dr Riley's eyes widened when she saw it, and her lips pursed, but she said nothing. He quickly searched through the photos and found the picture of Mandy Harris' driving licence. He pushed it forward to show Billy.

"This is Mandy, Billy. Do you know her?"

To his surprise, Billy moved his head to get a better look at the image. His eyes flicked up to Swanson and back down to the table. Dr Riley shifted slightly in her seat and stared at Bailey intently.

"Someone has hurt her, Billy. Mandy isn't okay, and we need to find out who wanted to harm her. Her sister is very upset."

Mentioning sisters was risky after what happened to both of his only a few months ago. But if it worked to get some information, then the risk would be worth it. But once again there was no reaction from Bailey.

"Her sister needs our help, Billy. Her name is Dotty. Dotty Foster. I'd really like to help both of them if I—."

But he stopped when he saw Bailey's head snap up. His eyes narrowed and the corners of his lips foamed with spit.

"Foster? Dotty Foster?" Bailey stammered as if he wasn't sure how to use his voice.

Swanson nodded slowly, unsure what to say or do. He hadn't expected Bailey to actually say anything.

"Do you know that name, Billy?" he asked.

Bailey's hands trembled on the table. His pale cheeks turned pink and then red.

"Billy?" Dr Riley said in a worried tone. "Are you okay?"

He jumped up so suddenly that he sent Dr Riley flying to the floor. Swanson pulled the pin from his alarm and the noise blared deafeningly through the room. Bailey roared and punched himself in the head repeatedly. He hurt himself with so much force that his face was covered in blood.

Swanson stood back helplessly as two nurses ran into the room and restrained Bailey's arms behind his back to prevent his fists hitting his face. He pulled against them but another two nurses followed quickly after and together they brought him out of the room and calmed him on the floor in the corridor. Dr Riley pulled herself up from the floor.

"Sorry DI Swanson, you will need to leave. Gary, take this man to reception please."

One nurse pulled back from Bailey, who sobbed on the floor, and waved at Swanson for him to follow. Swanson walked off in a daze. Bailey had actually spoken. He knew Dotty Foster. The big question was, what did he know about her to make him react like that?

8

Swanson

S wanson walked through the doors of the police station still confused, though at least his hunch was validated. He'd known it was too strong to be wrong. Billy Bailey did know something about the Mandy Harris case, or at least Dotty Foster. His reaction proved it. He might not know about her death or who did it, but something about that name being mentioned had upset him.

Now all he had to do was gloat to Hart that he'd been right. Then get Murray to authorise Summer to conduct a proper visit with Bailey. That would mean knocking on her office door again, and his cheeks felt hot at the thought.

He crossed the open office but hesitated amid the hustle and bustle. It wouldn't usually be so busy on a Sunday, but a murder case always grabbed everyone's attention. Even the lazy ones were out in force. All hands were on deck to find out what happened to Mandy Harris. He spotted Lisa Trent in the middle of a group of about five officers looking at some paperwork or pictures. The PR team had released a message to confirm a jogger found a body in Bell Woods, but they thought it to be a standalone incident with no immediate danger to the public.

If there was another person who belonged to Bailey's murderous group, someone he hadn't previously mentioned, then that statement wasn't true. There was a tremendous threat to the public still roaming around.

Fuck it. He needed to get over what happened yesterday and talk to Murray. Hart was fine about it. Murray might be too. He forced himself forward to cross the office and knocked loudly on her office door.

"Come in!" Murray called.

He pushed open the door but paused in surprise. Hart was already there, sitting across from Murray. Some of the pressure relieved a little. Her presence made it slightly less awkward somehow, and at least she wasn't in Murray's arms this time. He cleared his throat and willed his cheeks not to burn at the memory of yesterday as he took a seat next to her and faced Murray's icy gaze.

"Glad you're here, Hart," he started. "I just went to visit Billy Bailey."

"Bailey? Why?" Murray interrupted. He could've sworn her tone was sharper than usual. "I didn't give authorisation for a visit to Gold Bay."

"I had a suspicion he might know something. Call it a hunch. The visit was nothing official. It wasn't more than a quick hello. I'm here to ask for an official sign off for Summer to visit him. I'll go with—"

"Regardless, you shouldn't be going to visit him without authorisation from me," Murray said. "You know that's how cases get messed up at court."

"Well, I *knocked* yesterday to ask, but you were busy," Swanson snapped. "You did say to do what I wanted."

From the corner of his eye he saw Hart's face fall into her palm. Murray's expression fell into one of pure rage. The vein on her forehead bulged dangerously. It would have been enough to cause him to backtrack usually, but he stupidly continued.

"And I got a text from some anonymous number warning me not to go near him, so obviously someone doesn't want us to talk to him for a reason. With all due respect this is a murder case and as an experienced officer, I had a hunch to follow. It may have led to nowhere and I could've wasted everyone's time. But the hunch turned out to be correct and I'm here to ask to do an interview officially with our psychologist in tow."

Murray dropped her gaze and let out a long, heavy sigh as if trying to gather enough patience to answer him. "I know about the text. Hart mentioned it a few minutes ago. It sounds like they were clutching at straws and know nothing about you. It's too late to ask afterwards," she replied.

Was she really going to say no because she was embarrassed about yesterday? He opened his mouth to argue, and she placed one hand in the air to warn him to be quiet.

"But," she continued, "tell me what Bailey said. Summer visited him only last month, and she confirmed he still hadn't said a word since his sisters' deaths. She said he didn't even look up at her."

"He said nothing to me. Not at first. I asked him about Mandy Harris and said she needed help. I didn't mention that she was dead, but I showed him a picture of her driving licence and he actually looked at it. His eyes moved. Then I mentioned Dotty Foster, and he finally spoke."

Murray's lips pursed as if unimpressed, but Hart finally took her head out of her hands and looked at him curiously.

"What did he say?" she asked.

"He said her name. Dotty Foster's name," Swanson said.

Murray's eyebrows formed a dark scowl. "He repeated the name? Did he confirm he knew her or was that it? That's your reasoning for me to allow Summer to speak to him again?"

"That's the only thing he said. But when I confirmed her name was Dotty Foster, he lost his shit. He screamed and jumped up and knocked his poor doctor over. Who was basically a child by the way. A *child* doctor."

"They weren't that hard for him to knock over then," Murray replied. She was clearly unimpressed. "If that's all you have, Swanson, then my answer is no. There are too many other avenues to be explored."

"Like what?"

Murray looked at Hart and gestured wearily for her to speak.

"I went to see Dotty Foster with Trent," Hart said. "She said Mandy had a threatening ex-boyfriend who she only split with about four months ago. I thought it would be a good idea to find him."

"Sure. Let Trent find him and we can look into Bailey," Swanson replied.

"I literally just said no to taking the Bailey thing further, Swanson," Murray snapped.

He looked at Hart so she could back him up like she always did. Like they did for each other. Murray didn't often say no to both of them, and he knew they could convince her between them. But this time Hart said nothing. She clamped her lips shut and refused to look at him.

"Fine. I won't ask Summer to visit him if that's what you want me to do." He stood up and pointed directly at Murray. "But you've told the public there is no immediate risk to them,

61

and if another body turns up because there is *another* unhinged serial killer out there, then the public will slay you and want your job."

He turned to storm out. Before he even reached the door, Hart jumped up out of her seat and scrambled after him. She was right on his tail coming out of the door, but he took off through the crowds of busy officers milling around.

"Wait!" she called through the din. "Swanson! Slow down and stop being petty. I'll share what you've found out with the team. We can get some other opinions."

He stopped mid stride and twirled around. "You think I'm being petty? You're the one who didn't back me up in there. Either because you're embarrassed about what I walked in on yesterday or because you're too involved with your new girlfriend to disagree with her and stick up for me!"

"Keep your voice down," Hart spat under her breath. "That wasn't why I disagreed with seeing Bailey. You're fixated on him. The ex just sounds like a more likely problem. Please, let's go to your office for a chat. We can talk it through."

"No. You do as you're told and look into the ex-partner like a good girlfriend and leave me alone in peace for once."

Hart's face crumbled, and his regret was instant. But he couldn't stop himself. He had to get away. He walked furiously out of the office and ignored the guilt tugging at him. Another person might die because of their refusal to let him do his job and investigate the crime. He needed to talk to someone that would understand. He needed Summer.

First he went outside for a cigarette, inhaling the deep lungfuls of smoke until he'd calmed enough to speak to her. Even though Summer wasn't in the station today, he ate a mint and used alcohol gel on his hands before calling her. She'd quit a while back, and he would not be the reason she started smoking again.

She answered her phone fairly quickly, but he had to hold the phone an inch away from his ear thanks to the ungodly noise that came from it.

"Where the heck are you?" he asked. "I thought you'd be packing, but that is not the peaceful sound of throwing things into cardboard boxes."

"The packing is nearly done. I've been doing bits of it all month. Joshua and I needed a break, though, so we're at that new soft play centre. He's burning off energy and I might not have peace but I do have hot chocolate and cake."

"Soft play?" Swanson repeated the words slowly. So it was children's screams that were deafening him.

Summer laughed. "Yes. It's not a foreign word, Swanson. I think you'd love it. The bright lights that bare into your soul. The melody of overexcited kids hyped up on sugar. And the threat of danger whenever you try to move from your seat. There's even greasy chips and chicken nuggets. A toddler stole one of my chips, mind you. The cakes are all right, though."

"That sounds like just my cup of tea." He shuddered.

"Are you okay? You sound mightily pissed off. Or is it just the thought of the horror of soft play causing you issues?"

"I'm worried about this Mandy Harris case and the involvement of Billy Bailey. Neither Hart nor Murray are taking it seriously. I went to see him at Gold Bay this morning and he was just like you said at first. He didn't speak to me or look at me. But he showed an interest in checking a photo of Mandy Harris and then he went mad when he heard the name Dotty Foster."

"Recognition? So he actually spoke?"

"Don't get excited. Murray won't authorise you to visit again."

"What did he say exactly?"

"Yes. Well, he said the name Dotty Foster again and then lost his temper when I confirmed that was the name."

"Oh. Repetition is a sign of catatonia. It's called echolalia. Sorry, babe."

Swanson's heart fell. He'd been relying on Summer being the one person to back him up and help him figure it out. "But he looked at the picture of Mandy."

"It might remind him somehow of Marcie. Mandy and Marcie sound similar. He might have wanted to double check he was hearing right or he didn't hear you at all and the photo just captured his attention. Especially if it was on your phone? If so, the light might have caught his eye. I wouldn't look too much into it."

"What? Do you agree with Murray too? Has everyone lost their shit today or what? I know I was the only one there, but he clearly recognised the name. It wasn't a case of simple repetition."

"I'm not saying I agree with Murray, but if everyone is telling you the same thing, then you might be the one in the wrong," Summer snapped back. "Are you sure you're not just stressed about us moving in together?"

"What? Did you really just say that? This case has nothing to do with us moving in together."

"No, but you've been acting strange with me all weekend!" she insisted.

He opened his mouth to argue that of course he wanted her to move in. But then he thought about the anonymous text messages and Bailey's reaction to the photo.

Hart was so sure the person who sent them didn't know him at all. But what if they did? What if they knew where he lived? What if they were watching him and waiting for someone close to him to show up? Summer wouldn't listen. She'd think he was paranoid.

"Actually, maybe you're right. I don't know where my head is at. We should hold off for a week or so," he said sadly.

Summer didn't respond. The echoes of children's shouts were all he could hear.

"Summer? Are you still there? I just think it might be for the best to wait a few days at least."

"Fine," she replied softly, then the line went dead.

Great. He'd fallen out with both Hart and Summer. Who was going to be next? Aunt Barb? His mum? He lit up another cigarette and stalked over to his car. He knew one thing for sure; he wasn't going back to that damn station today. Hart and Murray could figure it out themselves.

9

Summer

Summer bundled a hyper Joshua into the back seat of the car and headed away from the soft play centre. She forced herself to focus on the road and not on Swanson's last words, though tears stung her eyes. She swallowed them back, refusing to cry in front of Joshua.

"Are we nearly at Daddy's house, Mummy?" he piped up from the back seat.

"Five minutes, baby."

"Are you sure you can't stay and watch my football practice today? I'm going to be really good. I'm going to score."

"Aw, I'm sorry but not today. I have to sort out a few things at home so you and I can watch a film together later, remember? There's mess everywhere at the minute."

Guilt tugged at her chest as she thought about how she was going to tell him they were no longer moving into the cottage. He'd been asking to live there since they first visited. The poor kid was desperate for a back garden to play football in.

"Only one more sleep until we move!" Joshua sang.

"About that, Joshy." She hesitated and cleared the lump in

her throat. "It might take a little longer than one sleep. We're not sure yet."

She glanced at him in the rearview mirror and her heart broke as his face fell. A renewed anger for Swanson filled her. It was obvious he wasn't ready to move in together despite being the one to ask. He'd been dropping small hints for a while—it would've been nicer for him to say it earlier rather than one day before they were supposed to move. Tears stung her eyes as they pulled up to Richard's house. She sniffed loudly and cleared her throat to get rid of them.

"Are you okay, Mummy?" Joshua's blue eyes were full of concern.

"Of course I am! Just a cough and a runny nose," she lied. "Come on, let's get you to your dad."

A few minutes later she was back in the safety of the car, and the tears fell freely on the drive back home. She'd already started thinking of how nice it would be to see the cottage as a home.

She remembered how excited she'd been to move into the flat with Richard and Joshua over two years ago. It was beautiful, but they'd had nothing but bad luck since moving in. One month later, Richard left to be with someone else. And it was barely past a year since her brother's ex-girlfriend, Marinda, had murdered a friend's mum and attacked Summer in the living room.

She wiped her eyes when she pulled up to the car park outside the colossal Jacobean building that housed their small home. Her visions had been full of dreams the first time she pulled up in that space.

The tears had stopped by the time she climbed the thirteen stone steps leading up to the entrance, though the lump still stuck firmly in her throat. The number of steps were the reason Mum had actually warned her it would be bad luck before they moved in. Why were parents always right when you didn't want them to be?

But even Mum didn't deny how impressive the 1800s property was. A famous architect named Joseph Danbury built the building as an asylum on a ten-acre site. The original chapel still stood down the road, and the words *ANNO DOMINI MDCCCLI* were engraved beautifully above the grand entrance doors. The exterior was certainly more elegant than any cottage. Blue Staffordshire stone detailed the red brick in a sectional pattern. One hundred feet above the doors was a striking old bell tower, complete with a red brick column on either side. The building continued at a right angle on each side at a much lower height. But Swanson's traditional stone cottage was full of character and far more homely.

As she made her way to the doors, she had that same eerie feeling she'd had last night that someone was watching her. She spun around to see if anyone had followed her from the car park, but there was nobody there. She peered out at the vast fields behind it, which separated the building from the A52. Again, they were empty. A shiver tickled the back of her neck.

She turned back to the door and shook the feeling away. The eeriness was likely a remnant of being followed by Marinda and Lucy. It had been dragged back to the forefront of her mind thanks to Swanson's texts. She opened up the main doors to the building and made sure she locked the door behind her.

The foyer was a little more luxury left over from the asylum days. The antique floor was pretty but cold in the winter, and a grand chandelier hung from the ceiling. She climbed the marble staircase that lined the left-hand side of the room. The space was empty, but she could still feel eyes were on her from somewhere.

She pushed open another door and jogged down the corridor to reach her flat, slamming the door hard behind her. Her heart pounded in her chest. Ridiculous when there was no one in the car park or the foyer.

But what happened with Marinda and Lucy had lived with her ever since. Even after their respective captures, the paranoia of those first few weeks was not something she wanted to relive. The simple act of going the same way as another person down the street had filled her with dread.

She shook off her heavy winter jacket and hung it up on the set of overflowing coat hooks to the right of the front door. Somehow, Joshua had ended up with five coats on there despite only ever wearing one. The living room was filled with neatly stacked and labelled cardboard boxes, and the sight of them made her want to cry some more.

She went to the kitchen for a glass of juice. One argument did not mean they wouldn't move in together. Swanson just had to get over his cold feet. That was all. Anyway, there were no boxes in the kitchen. Though the fridge was pretty bare and the empty cupboards didn't make her feel much better. As she sipped on the tangy orange juice and scrolled through her phone, a text from an unknown number popped up on her screen. Intrigued, she clicked on the message. Her heart soared when she read it, and her loneliness dissipated.

Hi, beautiful. It's Aarron. I'm back in the UK! Fancy a catch up?

10

Swanson

S wanson pulled up in the closest car park away from the station, which was a supermarket he often frequented for lunch. And the one where Summer was once kidnapped by a desperate patient. It was packed with shoppers getting their food bits in before the early Sunday close at 4 p.m., and he pulled up at the rear where few people wanted to park.

He thumped the wheel hard enough to make his palm throb with pain; he'd had to get away from that place. He needed a plan, and for once he really was on his own. Hart had never not backed him. Not really. They might argue but she always had his back against Murray. Thanks to their relationship that ship seemed to have sailed for now.

Then there was Summer. She needed to know the truth about why he didn't want her to move in yet. But she'd already been threatened and followed once by a patient. She didn't need to relive that experience if the anonymous texter found out about her. He imagined her reaction. She'd probably get freaked out and be scared in her own home again.

His phone rang, and he looked at it in disgust. He'd pissed

off almost everyone he knew, so why the hell it was ringing was beyond him. But it annoyed him even further when he saw Hart's traitorous name flash up.

He ignored her and let the call ring out on the front seat as he climbed out of the car for another cigarette. At least he could smoke for longer if Summer and Joshua didn't move in. He shivered as he lit the cigarette and sucked it in. Winter was rolling in quickly, and the crisp air was only just above freezing. His bare hands turned numb by the time he'd finished his cigarette, which was yet another reason to quit. He climbed back into the car, switched the engine back on and dialled up the heat.

He glanced at his phone. Six missed calls in the ten minutes he'd stood outside of the car. Something bad had happened. He grabbed the phone with a hundred scenarios flashing through his mind. Five of the missed calls were from Hart. The final one made his heart skip a beat. It was from his mother. That one was definitely bad news. He called Hart back first, not wanting to know yet what his mother wanted. Hart didn't even say hello when she answered.

"Swanson, please get back to the station. Now."

"What's happened?" he asked, his fist clamped shut so tightly it shook.

"I'll tell you when you get here. Just hurry."he racked

"Is it Summer? Tell me, Hart," he shouted, unable to keep his voice calm. He needed to know what was happening before he went anywhere.

She sighed loudly. "No. It's not Summer. She's fine as far as I know."

He racked his brain for what else it could be. "Tell me, Hart. Is someone hurt?"

"I wanted to tell you in person, but you're so bloody stubborn. It's your Aunt Barb."

The world stopped moving at that moment. He moved the phone away from his ear, unsure if he wanted to hear anything else. Each breath was strained as he tried to make sense of Hart's words.

"Swanson?" Hart's echo came from the phone. "Are you there?"

His jaw clenched as he put the phone back to his ear. Each word was a struggle to get out.

"What about Aunt Barb?"

"Her son has reported her as missing."

Swanson didn't respond. He hung up and threw the work phone back down on the passenger seat. It bounced off and landed on the floor with a heavy thud. He sped out of the car park, almost knocking over a woman with a pushchair who screamed some profanity at him.

He drove like a rally driver to the station. The years of police driver training at the beginning of his career paid off once again. The noise of many car horns and pissed off drivers followed him, but he didn't pay any attention to them as he smashed through the hectic weekend traffic. He abandoned his car somewhere in the rear car park and stormed inside, barging through the door so quickly he walked straight into Lisa Trent.

"Oh, Trent. Good." He didn't bother to apologise. "Where is Hart?"

"She's in the main office." Trent pointed down the other end of the corridor. "About your Aunt—"

He pushed past her and strode down the corridor. Aunt Barb's sing-song laugh filled his head as he walked and his fists curled. The threat in the anonymous text crossed his mind. This wasn't usual behaviour for Aunt Barb. She was a social butterfly and rarely alone. Her disappearance had to be related to the text. It was too coincidental that he received the message right before her son reported her missing.

The thought of something bad happening to such a beautiful soul because of his own fuck up made him shake with rage. By the time he reached the communal office to find Hart, he was ready to blow at the first person who looked at him.

But the chatter in the office lessened the second he walked in. Heads fell down to stare at paperwork or empty desks. The odd person was brave enough to throw a worried glance his way. But they were saved from his wrath as he spotted Hart at the end of the office. She was reading from a file and biting her lip nervously. He headed towards her and the surrounding chatter slowly resumed.

"Hart!" he called to get her attention over the noise, though his voice came out strange and hoarse.

She still recognised his shout, though, and her head shot up. The knot in his stomach tightened when he saw her facial expression. After working with her for so long, and in so many dire situations, he knew that look. She was scared.

"Here." She handed him a thin file limply. "It was called in earlier but someone else was dealing with it. I've only just heard about it."

He scanned the initial report. One of her sons, Gerald Mason, reported Barbara Mason missing from her Darley Abbey home right before lunchtime. Swanson's lip curled at the sight of his name. Ger was his cousin and had always been a pompous twat.

Aunt Barb was supposed to meet Ger for breakfast and didn't show up. She also didn't answer her phone when he tried to call. So Ger got worried and went to her house to check on her. He'd found patches of blood throughout the kitchen and hallway leading to the parlour type room where the back door was.

Hart was right to look worried, but this was Aunt Barb. She was a survivor and a force of nature. God help anyone who annoyed her, never mind kidnapped her.

"Can you help us complete the details?" Hart asked softly. "Her son was a bit upset. We tried asking him about her normal habits and other relatives but he just wants us to go out and magically find her with barely any information."

"That sounds like my idiot cousin all right. Of course I can help. I see her more than her sons do anyway. I saw her yesterday afternoon."

"You did? Where?"

"We went to Darley Abbey cafe after . . . before I went to see Dotty Foster."

Hart's cheeks turned a fiery shade of pink. She cleared her throat before continuing. "Was she okay?"

"Yes. She was normal. We each had a sausage roll. She had a cup of tea. A quick chat. Then I dropped her off right to her door. I watched her walk inside."

"So she has other kids then? Or a partner?"

"Yes. One other son who is just as up himself as Ger is. His name is Ronald Mason, and he lives down south near London. She doesn't talk to him as much as Ger and he doesn't visit often. She is single but does like to date. Her husband died years ago. He owned a company and she sold it to keep the manor."

"What happened to her husband?" Hart asked.

"He was killed in a car crash by a hit-and-run driver over fifteen years ago. They were never caught."

"Sorry to hear that, Swanson. What about her usual habits?

74

Enemies? You know the drill."

"She has a sister called Sandra Swanson that she doesn't speak to much." He felt Hart's eyes flick up to him. She knew Sandra was his mother. He remembered about the missed call from his mother. She must already know Barb was missing. "And she sometimes drives a blue Maserati Quattroporte, though she has an Audi too. She prefers to walk now that she's getting older. I'm going to her house now. Who's there at the minute?"

"You know it's not a good idea to go there yourself, Swanson." Hart placed a hand gently on his shoulder. "You're not allowed to meddle."

"You and Murray didn't listen to my concerns about that threat. If I'd meddled more, she might not be missing."

He shrugged off her hand and looked away from her hurt face. He couldn't handle sympathy at that moment. It wasn't useful and wouldn't help with finding out where Barb was. His phone buzzed, and he absentmindedly pulled it from his pocket. He stood up straight when he saw the sender: anonymous.

I warned you to stay away from Billy. Good luck finding your poor auntie. She puts up a good fight.

"Swanson?" Hart said anxiously. "What is it?"

Swanson's fingers trembled with rage as he clenched his fists. He tried desperately to cling on to a remnant of sanity. But the darkness fell, and he roared as he threw the phone across the room. The phone cracked off the wall and silence descended again. This time everyone stared at him. He could feel the eyes on his back.

"What the hell was that?" Hart ran to retrieve the phone, and her face paled when she picked it up.

"I'm getting Murray," she called and stormed off into Murray's office without knocking.

His breathing was as heavy as though he'd ran a marathon and the walls of the stupid building were closing in quickly. Everything in his being told him he had to get out of there.

He raced out of the station and into the rear car park. He rubbed his face hard and pulled out his cigarettes. His hand still shook as he tried to light one, but he managed eventually and felt better from the first inhale. It didn't take long for Hart to come flying through the door.

"Swanson! Christ, I thought you'd gone somewhere without me."

"I *am* going without you," he replied.

"The fuck you are! You shouldn't be going in the first place. You know that. I'm coming and that's final."

He rounded on her, making her step back against the wall. Her face contorted in confusion.

"You and Murray didn't believe me. You thought I shouldn't be worried about that text," he snarled again.

"Hey, I know you're hurting but you need to calm down. This isn't my fault."

"No? Wasn't it you who sided with Murray? You two are to blame for not taking this seriously."

"Don't be a dick, Swanson!" Hart stepped forward and pushed her face as far up to his as she could reach. "This happened because you ignored the text and went to see Bailey. You should've left it to someone else."

"It's not like I didn't ask you and Summer to go."

He was forced to step back as Hart pushed past him and walked over towards the station door.

"Yes. You're right. I should've listened to you. Clearly someone doesn't want us near Bailey. But I am listening now,

Swanson, and you need to listen too. Let *us* find her. *You* need to go home. Murray's sent an officer to watch over your cottage already. She is taking it seriously."

He snorted but let her walk back inside without another word. She wasn't needed anyway. Nor was Murray. Or Summer. He'd find Barb on his own, and whoever sent those texts had better be ready to suffer the consequences.

11

Summer

Summer woke up on Monday morning with a renewed energy and a newfound sense of peace. If Swanson didn't want her to move in, then that was fine. Let him sulk. She and Joshua could find their own cottage if needed. She had just about enough in her savings now to pay for a deposit.

She double-checked her phone. He still had made no effort to contact her. But she had a text from Aarron suggesting a time for their catch up.

Today at 10am? Where shall we meet?

With no work on Mondays at the station and Joshua in school, it was perfect timing. Screw Swanson and his moody face. Her fingers worked furiously as she texted him back and suggested the cafe down the road that had recently been renamed to *Claire's Cobs.*

She got showered and dressed before waking Joshua up for school. It was much easier to get ready alone than with an eight-year-old asking a million questions about life or moaning about whatever was happening at school that day.

She pulled on a smart work blouse with navy suit trousers.

She left her hair down, flowing freely around her shoulders, and only wore a small amount of makeup. Thanks to the winter weather she looked like a ghost without foundation in December, so no makeup was not a good look.

"You look pretty, Mummy!" Joshua beamed once he was awake and dressed for school. "Are you going to work?"

She laughed at his bright smile. "I'm seeing a friend for breakfast today."

"That's not fair! I have to go to school." He stuck out his bottom lip. "Can't I come with you?"

"How is it not fair? You get to see your friends every day at school. Come on. Get your shoes on."

She drove him to his small primary school, which was about a five-minute drive away, and then drove home and parked the car back at her flat. *Claire's Cobs* was a greasy spoon cafe around the corner from her flat. It was nice to walk there rather than drive, even in the cold. They made the best cheese toasties she'd ever had, even better than her own. They didn't mess up the cheese to bread ratio like she always seemed to.

She zipped up her heavy coat, pulled on a black woolly hat, and set off down the street. It was 9:45 a.m., and the roads had quietened since rush hour. The quaint cafe was hidden about ten minutes away from the main high street in what looked like a normal mid-terraced house. Though its colourful front door stood out from the other properties in blue and white, as did the sign above with *Claire's Cobs* in big blue letters.

Summer pushed open the door to the small jingle of a bell. The counter was at the back of the room, and she smiled hello at the two women behind it. Both women nodded to her without smiling and continued chuntering to each other in thick Derbyshire accents.

"Yes, duck. That's what I told her!"

"Ooh, these young'uns don't listen. In't it coad outside today."

She'd known their names since her second visit to the cafe—Bev and Roz. But had no idea which was which. Both were rotund with greying hair, roughly in their late fifties. They always wore the same blue and white chequered aprons and looked far too much alike for her to tell them apart.

The cafe was quiet as usual. Though it was a good job that it never got too busy. The building was small, and the kitchen itself was crammed into the back room. So there was not a lot of space in the seating area. It made it easy to see that Aarron hadn't arrived yet. Not that she'd expected him to be there. She was ten minutes early.

There was enough space to fit six plastic tables dotted around in three uneven rows of two, and only two of the tables were taken up. Each one by an elderly man. Both men wore suits and were quietly reading a newspaper to themselves.

Summer took a seat in the corner closest to the door and popped the coat and hat on to the empty chair next to her. The table was right in front of the large front window so she could see Aarron when he arrived. She didn't bother to read the well-worn menu and rested her arms on the table while she waited.

The chequered tablecloth, which matched the blue and white scheme, was cold against her skin. It was made of that cheap waterproof material. She sat back in the chair and folded her arms instead. As much as she loved everything that happened at this time of year, the icy weather was not for her. Bring on the summer warmth.

At 10:05 she was still staring out the window and waiting for a glimpse of Aarron's car. Bev, or Roz, had already been over to the table to take her order. She'd ordered two cheese toasties to be made for 10:20 in case he was late.

A movement across the street caught her eye. But it was a short person, not Aarron. This person had their hood pulled over their face and bent down fiddling with their shoes. But even so, she could tell it wasn't him. Aarron was tall and had a distinctive walk. The person continued to fiddle with their shoe for a minute and then continued on their way down the street.

By 10:30 she'd eaten her toastie and was eyeing up his. It would serve him right for being so late. She tried to call him again, but it went straight to voicemail. She grabbed his toastie and tucked in to more cheesy goodness. It was going cold anyway, and she eased her guilt with the fact he was so late. Though it didn't escape her that Aarron Walker was never usually late to anything.

12

Swanson

Swanson swallowed down another painkiller and rested his head against the steering wheel. The cold of the wheel somehow eased the fiery ache in his forehead. Lack of sleep made his headaches so much worse, and he desperately needed to think straight to figure out what had happened to Barb and where she was.

He prayed for the tablets to kick in quickly and looked down again at his notes so far. Barb was supposed to meet her oldest son, Ger, but didn't show. Which is unusual because she loved that idiot more than anything and let him walk all over her. Ger hadn't even answered his phone earlier, despite the fact he should be waiting for news from the police.

An icy feeling cramped his stomach, but he pushed it away. There was no chance she was dead. He had to keep hope that she was alive. She may be in her seventies, but she was larger than life and strong as hell. It would take a lot to bring her down.

He was grateful to hear his phone ringing to prevent his thoughts from turning dark, and grabbed it from the front seat. He looked at the screen and saw Ger was returning his call. He leaned his head against the steering wheel again. The man worked as a solicitor in conveyancing and was difficult to talk to at the best of times.

"Hi, Ger."

"Alex. Thanks for calling," Ger replied in his self-important voice. "Where is she?"

"That's what I was hoping you could help me with. I wanted to talk through the last couple of days and see if we can figure this out."

"Why do you people keep asking me to do your job for you? Please explain to me what you have done so far to find my mother?"

Swanson squeezed his eyes shut tight. It somehow helped to keep the rage inside.

"I promise you we're doing everything we can to find her, but the more information we can get the more likely that is."

"You've done nothing!" Ger raised his voice. Swanson squeezed the steering wheel tight with his other hand. "You're just as useless as the rest of them! Maybe you've done something to her seeing as you were always jealous that she wasn't your mother!"

"Be careful what you say next, Ger," Swanson replied in a low and dangerous tone.

"Is that a threat? Are you threatening me?" Ger raised his voice. "Have you even spoken to your own mother since I reported her sister missing or are you too obsessed with mine?"

"I'm simply telling you to shut the fuck up before you say something you regret."

"That's it! I want you off this case and I will be making a formal complaint about your conduct. We aren't children anymore, Alex. You can't just threaten to dunk me in the damn paddling pool anymore."

A memory of a snivelling little Ger came to Swanson. He'd caught the little shit trying to torture slugs with salt. He'd legged it to Aunt Barb when Swanson threatened to throw him in the paddling pool.

"What was that?" Ger squealed. "Are you laughing? My mother's missing, potentially seriously hurt somewhere, and instead of finding her you're laughing at me?"

Swanson realised a deep rumbling laugh was indeed coming from his own mouth. The memory of Ger's pudgy little legs and rotund tummy as he ran away made Swanson laugh out loud even more.

"That's it! You'll be off the case in the next five minutes!" Ger hung up and Swanson continued to laugh deeply until tears fell from his eyes. His laughter turned to heavy sobs, which racked his whole shoulders.

He did not know how long he was crying for, but eventually he wiped his face with his coat sleeve and took a deep breath. Ger was right about one thing, this was no time to fall apart. Barb needed him, and he would not prove Ger or his stepdad right.

He also needed to speak to his own mother. He downed a bottle of water first. Then stretched and prepared himself mentally to speak to her. Their relationship had gotten less awkward over the last year thanks to her leaving his stepdad, but it was still strange. He quickly hit Call on the phone before he changed his mind.

"Alex." He could hear the smile in her voice, and he had to admit it was nice having someone who was always happy to hear from him. Barb was the same. "Thank you for getting back to me. Ger rang me yesterday and I've been so worried. Have you found her?"

A ping of annoyance ran through him at the thought of Ger ringing her before he had. "No, Mum. We haven't. Did you speak to her last week?"

"Oh, dear. No, I didn't. I haven't spoken to her since her birthday in September. So that was—" He could almost hear her doing the mental maths through the phone.

"Three months ago," he answered.

"Yes. Ooh I didn't realise it had been so long. I had planned on dropping off her Christmas present soon."

Another ping of annoyance. "Really? What did you get her?"

"Well, nothing yet. I've been busy," she replied.

"Useless as ever," he mumbled.

"What was that, dear?"

"Nothing."

"I could call Greg? He could help to look for her."

Swanson's blood ran cold at the mention of his stepdad. "I thought you two didn't talk anymore," he replied.

"We aren't together but he calls the odd time. There's no harm in talking, is there?"

"That depends on your view of how he treats kids," he snapped as a childhood memory of Greg yelling at him came to mind.

You will be the death of your mother one day, Alex Swanson!

"What do you mean?" his mum asked, confused.

He pushed away the memory. She really didn't have a clue of half the things Greg said to him, and he certainly didn't have the mental energy to deal with telling her anything right now.

"Nothing. I need to go, Mum."

"Please call me if you find anything out, Alex. I know I'm not the best sister, but I really do love her and I am worried."

He hung up and stared out the window. Mum and Ger had been more useless than any relatives had ever been on previous missing persons cases he'd been involved with. It wasn't normal for a family to be so difficult. Though he'd had it easy compared to the likes of Billy Bailey and Marcie Livingstone.

Hart had not returned his calls all morning, and he wanted to stay far away from the station for as long as possible. When he'd visited that morning to find Hart, he couldn't bear the looks of pity as anyone he passed quickly busied themselves with a task or avoided him.

He needed to visit Barb's house, but it was crawling with other officers. Tonight would be better. He could look over everything in peace and see if anything was out of place that a stranger might not notice.

A message popped up on his phone, and his heart sank when he looked at the sender. Anonymous. He resisted the urge to throw the damn phone out of the window and opened up the message; this time it was an image.

The image was of a cafe he knew well. It was a place he'd eaten with Summer occasionally. And in the cafe window was a table where Summer liked to sit. In the image, Summer was alone at the table, looking out the window as if trying to spot something.

There was no text this time. But the threat from the image was clear. Summer was in danger and thanks to his own idiocy she had no idea. He slapped his hand hard against the steering wheel. She didn't even know about Aunt Barb going missing. Or the disturbing anonymous text messages. He quickly brought up Summer's phone number as he kicked the car back into gear to head to the cafe.

"Swanson what—"

"Get out of the cafe now," he yelled.

"What? Where are you?" she asked in an angry whisper.

"I'm on my way."

"You're on your way to the cafe? Do you want me to leave or not?"

He thought about Summer leaving the cafe and walking back to her flat alone.

"No! Actually, stay where you are. Are there other people in the cafe?"

She tutted loudly. "Make your mind up! I don't know what's wrong with you lately."

"Are there other people in the cafe? Yes or no?"

"Yes! Of course. Are you going to tell me what's wrong or not?"

"Good. Stay there. I won't be long."

He hung up and sped down Uttoxeter Road towards Mickelover where the cafe lay. Images of Summer being hurt by an unknown, hooded figure plagued his mind and blood pounded in his ears so loud it was hard to hear.

A woman in a Mini beeped her horn at him as he cut her off to turn left. He reached the cafe and abandoned the car in the middle of the road. He threw open the door and jumped out. Summer was standing outside on the street and looking at him with pure confusion.

"What the hell is going on?" she snapped. "I'm supposed to be meeting Aarron!"

"Aarron?" Swanson scanned the street as he ran across the road to greet her. It was empty. "What's he got to do with anything? He's on the other side of the world isn't he?"

"He messaged me last night to say he's back in England on a

visit. He wanted to meet and have a catch up."

He tried not to let his distaste for Aarron show. Not that he was jealous. The guy was just a weird idiot. An idiot who'd tried to date Summer right as Swanson met her. "Then where is he?"

Summer glowered at him, and a realisation hit him. They were supposed to be moving in together that day. She didn't yet know why he'd prevented it. No wonder she was so angry with him.

"He didn't show yet," she finally replied, exasperated.

"Yet? How late is he?"

Her eyes narrowed. "Late. Why is your car abandoned there?"

"Come on. Get in the car and we can talk."

"I'm not sure I want to talk to you." She folded her arms and bit her trembling bottom lip. He placed a hand on her cheek.

"Summer, look at me. I'm sorry. There's just a lot of stuff going on at the minute."

"I don't care." She sniffed loudly. "There's always some-thing going on with you."

"Hey." He grabbed her small hand instead. "Come with me. I'll tell you in the car."

"You don't get it, do you?" She snatched her hand from his grip and turned away. "I'm going home. Leave me alone."

13

Summer

Summer's feet stamped against the pavement as she stormed off in a fury. Tears stung her eyes, but she swallowed them down. Swanson couldn't see her cry. He was no good with emotions as it was.

"Summer! Please get in the car," Swanson called after her.

She didn't bother to respond or even turn around. It was bad enough that he'd refused to move in together without telling her why. But to then not contact her at all and turn up at the cafe telling her to get out—well that was something else. It didn't matter what his excuse was this time. There was always something.

Halfway back to her flat she rounded a corner, as did a vehicle that then slowed beside her. Her heart skipped a beat despite thinking Swanson was a paranoid mess. She glanced over and huffed in frustration. Swanson was following her home.

"What are you doing?" She stood still and yelled to him through the open car window.

"I'm just making sure you get home all right," he called. "Then I'll leave you alone."

She huffed and continued to walk down the street as he rolled beside her. Another car beeped its horn loudly, and she turned to see two cars trailed behind him.

"This would be a lot easier if you just got in the car," he yelled again.

Another car turned up behind to form a queue of three, and she couldn't help but laugh at the ridiculousness of him slowing down the whole damn street. And he called *her* the stubborn one.

"Fine!" she yelled back. "Let me in."

He pulled to a stop, and she walked around the car so she could jump into the front seat. She refused to look at him. Her anger at being ignored all night was still bubbling away.

"I'm only doing this to help those poor drivers stuck behind you," she muttered.

"And I'm only doing this to keep you safe."

"Is that why you ignored me last night?" she asked.

"I didn't ignore you."

"You didn't call me either. Who are you keeping me safe from?"

"Billy Bailey."

Summer finally turned to look at him, albeit with disbelief. "Bailey is locked away, Swanson. Marcie and Marsh are dead. What could Billy Bailey possibly do to me?"

"All I know is he recognised Dotty Foster and now her sister is dead. Something is going on, Summer. I got an anonymous message telling me to stay away from Bailey or else."

"What? Show me the message."

"Hang on a sec." They reached the small car park in front of Summer's flat and he pulled in next to her car. He grabbed his phone from his pocket, pulled up the messages option, and passed it to her.

"Look at the most recent messages."

Summer looked at the list of contacts he'd received messages from in the inbox, but there was no anonymous number.

"There's no anonymous messages here," she said, handing him back the phone.

"What? It's right here." Swanson scrolled through the messages himself. "I don't understand where it's gone."

"Swanson," Summer started softly and placed a hand on his thigh. "Are you okay?"

"No, Summer. They sent me a threatening message, and then another one with a picture of you alone in the cafe!"

"Well, I don't know what to say then. There's nothing in your inbox now."

"You deleted it!" Swanson spat. His sweaty forehead was turning red, and she could feel her own anger brimming at the surface, ready to spill over.

"I didn't delete anything!" she yelled back and pushed open the car door. She turned to him before getting out. "I think you should speak to Hart."

"*Somebody* deleted them."

She slammed the door and turned to walk off towards the flat.

"Summer!" His voice followed her. "My Aunt Barb's missing."

She stopped in her tracks and spun around. "What do you mean she's missing?"

"I got a threatening text and now she's missing. Get inside and call Hart if you don't want to speak to me. I gotta go."

With that he raced off out of the car park. Trust Swanson to reveal something huge and then run away. She stormed back up the unlucky thirteen steps to the main doors and shoved them open. She felt eyes on the back of her head and turned to snap at Swanson.

But no one was there. Just like before.

She swallowed and walked inside, again making sure she'd locked the main door. Sometimes people forgot to shut it properly. It was silly. Swanson was just making her paranoid. But she jogged all the way to her flat all the same.

Her chest burned by the time she made it upstairs. Once safely locked inside, she put a hand to her chest and took some deep breaths. An exercise routine was definitely needed.

She grabbed her phone and tried to call Aarron one last time. But instead of ringing out, an automated voice informed her the phone number had been disconnected.

She brought up social media instead and found Aarron there. He'd posted twenty minutes ago with a picture of him and his beautiful new girlfriend at a beach. She forced herself to read the caption.

Enjoying the Christmas sun in Shark Bay!

So he was still in Australia. Or he was in England and posting snapshots of memories. People did that sometimes. She commented underneath the picture.

Wow, looks great! Are you there today?

She also needed a conversation with Hart. May as well call her while waiting for Aarron to respond. Luckily Hart answered on the first try.

"Hi, Summer. Are you okay?" she asked in her usual sharp manner.

"Yes, fine. I'm worried about Swanson. He's been acting strange."

"Strange as in how?"

"He came to kick me out of a cafe when I was waiting for a friend and said something about anonymous text messages. He's obsessed with Bailey having something to do with this murder. Has his aunt gone missing?"

Hart sighed loudly. "Yes, she has. We're out looking for her now. He does act strange when he's upset, Summer. He won't say the words, but he needs you right now. His aunt's son has already been in touch saying Swanson threatened him and he's not to work on the case."

"Ger? I've heard about him. Is Murray going to kick him off the case?"

"She could try, but we all know he'd ignore her. Try calling him, Summer. He needs someone."

The guilt sat heavy in Summer's stomach as they hung up. All this time she'd been moaning about Swanson not being there for her when she hadn't been there for him. And when he opened up to her at last she'd accused him of losing his marbles and stormed off.

She *had* to find him. Even if it was just to sit with him while he talked through theories about where Barb had gone. A phone call would be a good start. Though when she went to bring up his number, a new comment on social media from Aaron flashed up on her phone. He had responded to her question, and his answer made her feel sick.

Yes! We're here all weekend. Beautiful isn't it?

14

Swanson

S wanson pulled up outside Aunt Barb's building in a beautiful part of the leafy village named Darley Abbey. It was so serene and pretty in parts that he couldn't imagine anything bad ever happening here. Barb lived in an enormous house that he often jokingly called her manor, much to her annoyance. He'd parked across the road. His plan to wait until nighttime hadn't worked. He couldn't wait any longer to look around. If he didn't figure out who was behind this quickly, then god knows what might happen to Barb.

Though he should have stayed with Summer to make sure she stayed safe. She was so damn stubborn sometimes. It would have helped to tell her the full story from the beginning, but Summer had been followed and stalked before. It wasn't something he wanted to worry her with again without proof. As if reading his mind, a text from Summer popped up on his phone.

Aarron isn't in England. He's still in Australia. Someone was pretending to be him to meet me. I'm fine, though. Go look for Barb and let me know how I can help. I understand and I love you.

Goddammit. This was turning out to be the worst week ever. He brought up Hart's number.

"Yes, Swanson?" she snapped. "You don't need to keep ringing me. I will let you know if I find out anything. What did you say to Ger by the way? Have you spoken to Summer? And where are you?"

"Never mind that. Summer and Joshua being targeted next. Are you in the station? Is Murray there? I need a car to go watch her."

Hart let out a string of curses that would put a sailor to shame. "Hang on."

The line went silent, and he watched the people who were in and out of Barb's house. People who didn't know her. Strangers who didn't care, not really. She was another case to them. It didn't affect their lives. He clenched his fist. It took everything in him not to get out of the car and tell them to get the hell away from her home.

"Done." Hart's voice reappeared. "She's sending a car now and is going to request that Summer come into the station for a bit. She agrees it might be useful to get her to talk to Bailey about Dotty Foster. Murray wants me to send a car for you too. She's asked someone to watch the cottage."

"Asking Summer to come in might put her at more risk. If they know she's involved in the case, then it might up the ante."

"They probably already know, Swanson. And if she's already being watched then she's better off with us then alone at home. Now will you please tell me where you—"

He hung up and climbed out of the car. He flashed his ID badge to a young officer standing guard outside the property and walked straight inside. It was surreal seeing everyone in her beautiful home. He took his time to walk around and tried to see it in a new light. Not as a safe space to spend time with the one adult figure he'd always adored, but as a potential crime scene.

It still smelled like her, and he breathed in deeply. He pushed the memories aside and did what he would do with any potential crime scene. He strolled in and out of each room looking for anything out of the ordinary. Nobody paid much attention to him; they focused on their own jobs for the day.

It wasn't their relative's much loved home. It was simply another day in the office. But there was nothing out of the ordinary that he could spot. It looked the same as it did every time he visited, bar the police paraphernalia around the spots of blood.

There was a box of Christmas decorations in the unused office that stopped him in his tracks. Sticking out of the top was the ancient angel that she always asked him to stick on the top of the tree for her since she couldn't reach it herself. He reached for it and fingered it gently. Next to the box of decorations lay two presents, both neatly wrapped in snowflake covered paper. One was a large, square box. The other was smaller and shaped more like a book. Before he could help himself he'd bent down to turn the tags over. The box was addressed to him and Summer in Barb's neat, cursive writing. The smaller one was for Joshua. He closed his eyes, then forced himself back to his feet. The angel was still in his hand, and he sat it on the desk, not able to bear the idea of it being in the dark box forever.

But an unusual mark on the desk caught his eye. An image someone had engraved onto it with a sharp knife or something similar. It was recent, and the indents were still filled with fresh dust. His pulse raced as he realised what it was.

He blew the dust away and snapped a picture of the carving

with his cell phone. It was all the evidence he needed. They'd found the same mark on Charlie Marsh's skin and again on Marcie Livingstone's arm. It was their mark. The mark of the family of serial killers.

15

Swanson

Swanson returned to the police station with a renewed sense of determination. Aunt Barb was alive. He could feel it in his bones. She wasn't dead, despite the mark. Few people would be stupid enough to kill an officer's relative.

Although not many would carry out the kidnap of one either. If they wanted his attention, they had it on full blast.

He'd make sure they regretted it too.

He walked down the main corridor and heard familiar low voices coming from the kitchen. His step slowed, and he stopped right before the open door.

"He hasn't answered my calls since," Summer whispered. "I don't know what to do or how to help him."

"Don't worry." Hart attempted to whisper, but it wasn't her strong point. "He'll be okay. He's probably looking for Barb. We might find him at her house. Let's check."

Before they caught him ear wigging, he strode into the kitchen as if he hadn't heard a thing. Summer smiled in relief. Hart gave him a nasty scowl.

"Where the hell have you been? No. Never mind. I don't want

to know. Can you not make us worry about you as well, please," she snapped. "We've got enough on trying to find Barb."

"I knew you loved me really," he replied.

"I'm sorry about earlier, and that I didn't believe you about the messages," Summer piped up. She looked away sadly. "I didn't want to believe it was true. The thought of being followed again . . ."

She trailed off and Swanson stood awkwardly in the doorway, unsure if she wanted him to comfort her or to go away. It wasn't long ago that she was yelling in his face. But her anxiety about being followed was the exact reason he hadn't told her about the messages in the first place, and seeing her scared face made him feel ten times more guilty than he already did.

"Forget it," he replied. "It doesn't matter now as long as you're safe. I'm sorry for not telling you earlier. But look at this."

He held out his phone with the image of the tattoo engraved into the desk. He watched as Hart's face fell. Summer looked confused.

"What is it?" she asked.

"Charlie Marsh's tattoo," Hart whispered. An actual whisper this time, and he looked at her in surprise. He'd never known she was capable.

"Oh, yes. I've heard about this tattoo that got them caught," Summer replied. She looked over at Hart as she spoke. Her face had paled significantly. "Are you okay, Hart?"

Hart hesitated, but after a moment she nodded. "Yes. Yes. I'm fine. Where was this, Swanson? Where did you find it?"

"In Aunt Barb's study. Someone engraved it on the desk. It's new. The dust was still settling inside the grooves. The person who took her did this. I know they did."

Hart swallowed hard and nodded again. "Okay. So we need a plan then."

"What did Marsh tell you about this tattoo exactly?" Swanson asked. "You never told me properly."

"Marsh was a foster kid. Her foster parents didn't treat her well at all. You know that. She said her stepdad, Lee Torrent, tattooed this mark on them all. At first he said it meant he owned them. But Marsh killed him, so he isn't around to ask. Marsh didn't know what happened to his murder investigation with the police after. She never wanted to look it up."

"Let's look it up now. It might mention something about the tattoo," Swanson replied, walking out of the kitchen and taking a left towards the communal office. It might be noisy but it had lots of computers.

The two women followed him down the corridor and they each grabbed a computer at a row of desks on the far right. It wasn't overly busy for once, much to Swanson's happiness. Although it was probably because they were all too busy destroying Barb's manor.

"I'll look into Lee Torrent," Hart said. "Swanson, you look into the foster mother. Her name was Dorothy Tilly. Summer, can you look into Charlie Marsh's background, please? I could never bring myself to do it."

"Sure," Summer replied. "I only have clearance to do basic searches, though."

"That should be enough," Hart replied.

They busied themselves in silence with their respective tasks, but it didn't take long for Hart to pipe up again about Lee's record. She almost growled as she read his file.

"This guy was the worst. He had a record for indecent exposure and having sex with two 15-year-old girls as well as beating his missus numerous times. They should have locked him up for life. He has the same tattoo. It's listed as being on his left wrist. A quick search also brought up his death. Stabbed to death twenty-five years ago. No suspects listed. It doesn't look like they did much to find out who did it. Certainly no foster kids were listed, which is weird. You'd think if the foster witch was dead too then it would list something about trying to find them."

"They listed her as a murder here. Someone stabbed her too. Same time, same place as Lee Torrent," Swanson mused. "No tattoo listed, though. Makes sense if he was the one to tattoo them I guess."

"What about you, Summer?" Hart asked. "Find anything else out?"

Swanson looked over at Summer. Her face was white and her eyes bloodshot. She swallowed hard and cleared her throat.

"Ahem. Probably best not to go into detail." Her eyes flicked over to Hart and back to the screen. "But she got arrested once. They suspected her of being involved with the death of a man and a woman. Her parents, I think. The last thing listed here is an address for one Dorothy Tilly. No one made any visits after they dropped her off. That's weird, isn't it? I know it's much tighter these days. But I'm sure foster kids got at least semi-regular visits even back then. It lists the social worker as Nadene Andersson. There was also a police officer involved from Leicester in the initial case. He's listed as being present at the drop off to Tilly's house. He was called Ben Jackson."

"I wonder if any of this is familiar to Dotty Foster. It might be linked," Swanson replied. He looked at Hart, who was chewing furiously on her bottom lip. "What did she say when you called her yesterday?"

"Oh, we arranged to meet later today. She didn't want to talk over the phone. I'll ask her about Lee and Dorothy and the tattoo symbol."

"Great. What time?" Swanson asked.

"About six o'clock. After she's finished work."

"She's still going to work? Wow. I don't think I could function if someone murdered my sibling so horribly," Summer said.

"It's strange how some people react," Hart replied. "Sometimes they need to keep going. It can help."

Swanson looked at the time on his phone. "That's five hours away. So it gives us time to look into Nadene Andersson and Ben Jackson seeing as they are the only two who are hopefully still alive."

"Okay. Let's go," Summer replied, taking Swanson in arm. "Let's figure it out together. Yeah? No more hiding things."

"You need to come with me, Summer," Hart piped up. "Swanson can't do it. He's related to the missing person. It could mess the investigation up if it goes to court."

"When," Swanson interrupted. "*When* it goes to court."

Summer nodded and let go of Swanson's arm. "Yes, *when*. And fine. I'll go with Hart. But we won't have time to visit both before Dotty Foster."

"Go and see Nadene Andersson, and I'll find someone to visit Ben Jackson. As an ex-police officer he'll be easier to chat to," Swanson said. He looked around the office and nodded towards the corner. "Trent will probably do it. She's been helping already, and she was the one who spotted something wasn't right with Marsh."

"Swanson!" Summer scolded and looked over at Hart, who let out a defeated sigh.

"No. It's fine. If you want someone to be interrogated, she's the one to do it right," Hart agreed. "But don't bloody go with her, Swanson. You know you can't."

She shot him a warning look, and he shuffled uncomfortably. Judging from Hart's piercing glare, it must have been clear by the look on his face that he was considering it.

"It won't stand in court if you keep interfering. I can't imagine how you're feeling, but don't you want these bastards to go down?" Summer asked.

"And don't forget your cousin, Ger," Hart said.

"What about him?" he asked.

"Oh, I thought I'd said. He wants you off the case. He said you threatened him."

Swanson snorted. "I did no such thing. He's just an idiot."

"Nothing to do with me. He demanded to speak to Murray. So you're probably best off keeping out of her way too."

He cracked his knuckles in frustration. Summer stood and Hart quickly followed her.

"One of us will call you as soon as we're back," Summer said.

"*On* the way back, please," Swanson replied.

"Sure," Hart said. "Just keep your arse in the station. Probably best in your office away from Murray. Then it's the safest place for you, but it's also what's best for the case."

They walked away before he could say anything else. An empty feeling overcame him as he watched them leave, and the temptation to follow was hard to resist. But as if she could sense his plans, Murray stuck her head out of her office door. He quickly bobbed down by the side of the desk and watched her through the gap in the table. Her head moved from side to side as she searched for something, probably him, and then she disappeared and closed the door.

He snuck out of the room and down to his own shabby office. It was dark and peaceful, and for want of something better to do, he sagged into his comfy, old chair. For once it had stayed in the right position.

He stared at the paperwork still splayed out on his desk. Most of it he recognised as his own notes that he'd forgotten to put away, but on the top of the paper lay a map he hadn't seen before. It was a map of Darley Abbey, and someone had circled a big area right around Aunt Barb's house.

16

Summer

Walking through the station to the car park felt different than usual. Like there was an impending doom around the corner and she needed to be careful. It was a heavy sense of anxiety, probably caused by being followed all over again. No matter how hard she tried, she could not shake the feeling that someone was watching her everywhere she went.

"Let's go in my car," Hart announced as they reached the car park.

Summer agreed. She was happy not to drive. Her own car was a mess anyway thanks to Joshua. How he got crumbs all over when he only ever sat in the same seat was a mystery she'd never been able to solve.

Hart had parked her car haphazardly two rows down from the entrance. Summer climbed into the passenger seat and punched the postcode into the sat nav system. Hart sat back and chewed her lip, looking deep in thought.

"What are you thinking so hard about?" Summer asked.

"I was thinking that Nadene Andersson is very unlikely to

still be at this address and Swanson has possibly sent us down a rabbit hole."

"Possibly," Summer agreed. "But I think it's worth checking it out."

"I guess so. As long as he hasn't sent us somewhere so he can do something else without us knowing."

"Like what?"

"Who knows with him? His head isn't in the best place. Let's go, then."

Nadene's listed address was a good hour away from Derby. She apparently lived in the small town of Oadby, four miles from the city of Leicester. They spent a lot of the drive along the motorway in silence, each lost in their own thoughts. As they arrived, Summer watched the busy main road out of the window. The town was a pretty mishmash of modern buildings and period homes.

"I'm sure this is where the university is based," Hart muttered as she squinted at the sat nav.

Swanson had mentioned she needed glasses a few times but refused to acknowledge it. There was a spare pair of reading glasses sitting in Summer's handbag, but she thought better of offering them to Hart.

"There's Brocks Hill Country Park too," Summer replied instead. "That's a nice place."

"I think that's where this house is actually," Hart said. "It looks very close to the park."

They continued the drive down Wigston Road to Brocks Hill Country Park. The views changed to larger detached houses that were half hidden from view thanks to the surrounding greenery. "It's down here somewhere." Hart pulled down a narrow country lane barely wide enough for two cars. "I hope a bloody truck doesn't come this way. Keep your eyes peeled for a house."

The lane wasn't too long, and at the end was a huge, detached period property. It wasn't unlike a mini version of the building Summer's flat resided in; except someone owned this whole place. Despite the age of the property, the surrounding land was modernised. The drive was tarmac, and mature trees bordered a perfectly manicured lawn. It wasn't to Summer's taste, but someone had looked after it well. Hart whistled through her teeth.

"This is not the kind of house I'd expect a social worker to live in," she mused as she parked up at the end of the driveway.

"No," Summer agreed. "I know what they get paid, and it isn't enough for anything close to this."

"Maybe she won an inheritance," Hart muttered as she got out of the car and took a moment to stare at the impressive building.

It was the kind of place that was beautiful to look at, but it was hard to imagine actually living in it day to day. It looked lonely without a big family to fill it up. And it would be a pain in the ass to look after properly and keep in such good condition. They walked up together to the front door, and Summer knocked loudly. Hart quickly stepped to the corner to look down the side of the building.

"I think that's actually Brocks Hill Park past the back," she whispered.

Summer didn't have time to respond as the front door flew open and she took a step back. A tall woman appeared in front of them. She wore square framed glasses and had dark hair pulled back into a ponytail. Her face was hard, and she glared at them as if they'd interrupted something very important. She looked nothing like the soft image Summer had in her head of a gentle social worker. Hart quickly flashed her ID.

"Hi, I'm Detective Inspector Rebecca Hart, and this is my colleague Summer Thomas. We're here to speak to Nadene Andersson, please."

"That's me. How can I help?"

The woman's face softened, and she plastered on a bright smile. So it really was Nadene. She looked nothing like Summer had expected. Although she looked great to say she must have been in her sixties. Her skin was smooth and her eyebrows didn't move. That would be quite a feat if she'd had a long career in a job as stressful as a social worker. But it was clear she'd had expensive work done to her face. That was difficult to do on a social worker's budget, just like keeping such a gigantic period home.

"Perfect. Lovely to meet you. Can we come in, please?" Hart asked. "It's nothing to worry about. We wanted a quick chat with you about an old case you were involved in."

"Sure!" Nadene pulled her smile even wider and waved them inside. "Come straight in through here and we can have a chat in the kitchen."

The pair stepped past her and on to the polished Victorian tiles of a grand entrance hall. A dark oak stairway lay to the right of the hall, and vintage patterned plates hung from the otherwise plain white walls. An ancient rocking horse caught Summer's eye and almost made her step right back outside again. It had discoloured and cracked in places, and its remaining dull eye watched them closely.

Nadene closed the front door behind her with a thud and led them through the hall and into a door at the end that opened up into the kitchen. A bit like the town it was a part of, the house was mismatched with contemporary design and older style ornaments. And whilst she'd decorated the hall and stairs as Summer expected, the enormous kitchen was different altogether.

It still had the bright white walls of the hallway but a marble island dominated from the middle of the room, and each wall was lined with sleek, modern black units.

Nadene ushered them through the kitchen to another vast room. She pulled out two cream chairs from a solid oak dining table that was almost as long as the room itself. Nadene fiddled with a silver locket around her neck as she took a seat at the head of the table.

Hart sat closest to her, and Summer followed her lead and took the remaining seat pulled out by Nadene. She smiled at Nadene gratefully, though the chair was so high-backed that it forced her to sit up awkwardly straight.

"Would either of you like a drink?" Nadene asked.

"No," Hart replied quickly.

Her face was harsher than usual, and it took Summer a minute to realise what was wrong. She could've slapped herself for not realising earlier. This woman had delivered Charlie Marsh into the hands of a monster as a little girl and never checked on her again. Marsh's terrible life was the fault of Nadene Andersson doing a shitty job as a social worker while she lorded it up in this beautiful home.

"Are you still practising as a social worker, Nadene?" Hart asked.

Nadene shook her head gently with a sad smile. "I retired three years ago."

"I see. The case I wanted to talk to you about is from quite a long time ago."

"That's okay. I remember most of them. I'd recognise a lot in the street if I bumped into them." She smiled proudly.

"This case involved a girl who you delivered to a foster carer called Dorothy Tilly."

Nadene dropped her smile instantly, and her face paled visibly. She swallowed hard before trying to speak again.

"Oh, dear. I remember poor Dorothy Tilly. They found her stabbed to death by the last child I brought to her. Evil little thing she was."

Hart opened her mouth to speak, but Summer quickly reached under the table to squeeze her thigh and put her off so she could jump in.

"Who was this little girl?" Summer asked.

"Oh, I remember her well. The child was called Charlotte Marsh," Nadene replied using air quotes around the word *child*.

Summer had visions of having to hold Hart back from Nadene by the time she'd finished talking about Marsh. Hart opened her mouth to say something, but Summer quickly jabbed her in the ribs. Nadene continued in a horrified, hushed tone.

"She killed her own parents."

"No. She didn't," Hart snapped.

Nadene was either undeterred by Hart's cheeks turning slowly red or didn't notice. She carried on in her dramatic low voice.

"They never proved it of course. She was clever. But Dorothy Tilly was a saint. She took on the most troublesome cases. She had a heart of gold. I don't know how she did it but she'd turn those naughty children around in no time."

"Did you visit and ask how she turned them around?" Hart asked, each word dripping with venom. It crossed Summer's mind that maybe Swanson would have been better coming along than Hart, after all.

"Yes, of course. At this point Dorothy already had a young lad called Bobby—"

"There's no record of you visiting Charlotte Marsh after dropping her off?"

"Oh, this was the olden days, dear. They didn't record everything word for word back then like they have to now. That's partly why I left. All that silly paperwork."

"Also, it was Billy that Dorothy had, not Bobby," Summer said. A feeling of protectiveness washed over her. Despite his crimes, he was little more than a baby when Nadene knew him.

"Oh, yes. That was it. Billy. He was always in trouble too. Such a strange boy. He refused to say a word to me, but yet again Dorothy sorted him out. He'd set his own stepdad on fire." She whispered the last sentence. "But being with Dorothy turned him into a quiet and respectful young man. He scarpered after she was murdered. I'll always feel guilty for dropping that little witch off with them. She was the type who should've been killed at birth."

"Dorothy Tilly was an abuser," Hart spat.

"She may have been tough, dear, but you didn't see what she had to put up with. You didn't meet those kids."

"She let her boyfriend rape them," Hart continued. "He made them touch each other."

Nadene's cheeks turned pink. She narrowed her eyes at Hart before replying.

"A lady like her would never do that! I'd have heard about it already if that was the case."

"He even took pictures of what he made them do to each other. It's all evidenced in his file. You can't deny it."

"Well," Nadene spluttered as she tried to find the words to

say. "That was probably the girl coming on to him and Billy and asking him to take pictures! She always knew that the kids she took in would murder her if she wasn't tough enough on them and she took that risk and lost. She should have been more tough on those brats. I doubt a confident young woman like yourself would even *dream* of taking such kids in and god knows where they ended up. In prison probably."

"If kids like that end up in prison then it's a failure of people like you." Hart stood up and turned away. "And Charlotte Marsh is dead."

"Good riddance," Nadene muttered under her breath.

Shit. Summer's eyes widened, and she stood quickly to put herself in front of Hart.

"She died saving many lives," Hart yelled, her eyes bloodshot. "More so than you and your evil, abusive foster carers, you useless, hard-faced, fucking bitch."

"Out. Now." Summer pushed Hart to turn her around and frogmarched her through the kitchen and into the hall.

"You can't speak to people like that! I hope you know I'll be making a complaint about this!" Nadene's shaky voice followed them as they walked out the door, though she didn't dare to walk after them.

One look at Hart's face and Summer didn't blame her. She pulled open the front door and pushed Hart through it. She stood back as Hart grunted and kicked a nearby tree. Then leaned against it, panting.

"Do you feel better?" Summer asked.

"She's a sick fucking bitch!" Hart muttered. She finally walked away from the tree with her hands planted firmly on her hips. Summer stood strong in between Hart and the front door.

"Yes. She is. Now, come on. Do you need me to drive or are you going to calm down? I'm happy to drive."

"I'll drive," Hart replied.

She unlocked the car doors and made her way over to the vehicle. Summer followed once she was absolutely sure Hart was not about to run behind her and back inside the house.

"Fine. You drive. Just try not to kill us, okay?" Summer climbed into the car next to Hart. "You drive erratically enough when you're in a good mood."

"Jesus, Summer. You're even starting to sound like Swanson," Hart replied, her face lined with a faint smile.

"I wonder what he'll think about all this," Summer muttered.

"Let's just tell him when we're back. He's hard enough to monitor face-to-face."

"Fine," Summer agreed, hoping against hope that Swanson was thinking a little more calmly by the time they got back to the station. She couldn't have both of them losing it over this case. They usually kept each other in check. Aunt Barb's life may depend on it.

17

Swanson

Swanson traced out potential routes of escape as he scoured over the physical map of Derby someone had laid out on his desk. He focused on the Darley Abbey area, where they had put a circle around Barb's house, and tasked himself with checking out where possible CCTV cameras might help him find out where she went. He was so engrossed that a knock at the door made him jump, which caused his pencil to fly across the map and mark out a random line. He cursed under his breath before calling them to come in. The door pushed open gently, and Lisa Trent appeared with a tentative smile.

"Oh, you got my map."

"You left this? I thought…" he trailed off as he realised his paranoia was getting the better of him. Anon was winning.

"Thought what?" Trent pushed. She had a look of concern that immediately made him want her to leave.

"Nothing. I just thought someone else had left it. How can I help?"

"Are you free for a chat? I just got back from speaking with

Ben Jackson."

"Sure. Grab a seat." Swanson nodded to the chair that had appeared from nowhere a few months ago.

He was pretty sure Hart had snuck it into his office against his will. Though she vehemently denied it.

Trent re-tightened her dark ponytail as she walked. It crossed his mind how annoying it must be having that much hair. He couldn't imagine anything less practical. She sat on Hart's chair and cleared her throat nervously.

"I wish I had something pivotal to tell you, but he didn't give me much, Swanson. I'm sorry. He was a very nice guy and worked for Leicester Police. He retired a couple of years ago now, though."

Swanson lowered his gaze and pursed his lips. He had expected little to come of it, but a surprise would have been nice all the same.

"What did he say about Marsh's foster case?"

"He said he doesn't really remember it."

"Did he know the social worker? What of Billy Bailey?"

"No. He doesn't know of Bailey or Livingstone by name."

"Hm. Thanks for doing the interview, Trent. I appreciate it."

"No worries. Anything else I can do to help?"

"You could check out these CCTV possibilities." He handed her the map with his markings around Darley Abbey.

"Sure. I'll take it through now. And, Swanson, I am really sorry about your aunt."

"She's not dead yet," he snapped.

Trent opened her mouth as if to speak more, but swiftly closed it and nodded sadly. She stood and left the office without another word. She closed the door softly behind her and he picked up a pen from his desk and threw it at the door. It bounced off with a pathetic ding that made him feel even more helpless. He couldn't stand not knowing. It was his responsibility to save Aunt Barb, and he didn't even know where to start looking.

What if she was dead? Or what if she was still alive somewhere, desperately waiting for him to save her but knowing he'll never find her?

He couldn't decide which was worse.

The door flew open again. This time it was Hart, with Summer not far behind, and she didn't bother to knock. They were actually becoming a great pair. If they worked out, Hart might leave him to work alone sometimes.

"Come in," he said in his most sarcastic tone as Hart took a seat. Her face was red and her hair unusually dishevelled. Summer perched on his desk. She'd probably add her own bloody chair in here soon too.

If she ever forgave him for saying he didn't want to move in together yet.

"We just got back. That social worker is a nasty piece of work," Hart spat. "And she was about as useful as a chocolate teapot when it came to finding anything out."

"Did anything at all come out of it?" Swanson asked.

"Not really," Summer replied. "Other than her making a formal complaint about Hart's conduct."

Swanson sighed and raised his eyebrows at Hart. "What did you do this time?"

"Nothing. I didn't do *enough*. You didn't hear what she said about Marsh. Poor Charlie was just a kid. Nadene Andersson deserved far worse than what I gave her today." Hart scowled.

Clearly it was time to change the subject.

"Okay. What did she actually say then? You still haven't told me."

"Just that our Marsh was evil as a kid. She had cold eyes. Whatever that means. Andersson was glad that she's now dead. She thinks Marsh murdered her own parents. She remembered Bailey and said he set his stepdad on fire. But that was it."

"What did she say about Dorothy Tilly?" Swanson asked. "There has to be a link somewhere in all this mess."

"She said Dorothy Tilly was great with the more disturbed kids and turned them into compliant and quiet, easy to deal with shells of themselves. She never asked how."

"She actually said that?" Swanson asked. "In those words?"

"No. *I* said that," Hart replied. "She beat them into submission whilst her boyfriend raped and abused them. I told the social worker that. She said Marsh probably came on to Lee Torrent and asked for it and Billy asked for the pictures to be taken."

Swanson's lip curled. Her words made him feel physically sick. Those kinds of cases never got easier in this job. Murder was easier to deal with than kids being tortured or abused.

Unless it was his aunt.

"Let's look at the facts then," Summer piped up. "Torrent is dead. Tilly is dead. Andersson was useless. And Ben Jackson?"

"Was useless with Trent. She's checking out CCTV possibilities but Jackson knew nothing really," Swanson replied. "So we're back at square one."

The three stayed quiet, each looking down at the floor and trying to think of their next steps. After a minute his phone lit up from the middle of the desk. Hart saw it first and, nosy as ever, pulled it towards her to check what it was.

"It says anonymous." She pushed it over to him and he scooped it up from the desk.

"Thanks for checking, Hart," he replied sarcastically. She rolled her eyes, and he looked down at the phone.

Did you like the clue I left on poor Barb's desk?

The bastard was taunting him. He turned his phone around to show Summer and Hart the screen. Summer looked at him sadly, and Hart cursed.

"Well, at least you know you're one step ahead of them," Hart said.

"Am I? I feel one step behind."

"You already saw the mark on the desk," Summer replied. "You're ahead of them and close to figuring them out."

His phone beeped again, and all three of them tried to crowd around the phone.

"It's anonymous again," Swanson muttered as he opened up the text.

You missed the other clue. Dogs love parks, don't they?

"The other clue?" Hart asked. "Where was that?"

"Park," Swanson muttered. He racked his brain trying to think of where the park might be. "Darley Abbey Park?"

"Got to be worth a shot," Hart replied. "Let's see what we can find."

18

Swanson

D arley Abbey Nature Reserve was around the corner from Aunt Barb's house. It was also where their regular meeting spot was situated, and the last place he saw her before dropping her off at home. It was a pretty park that offered sprawling greenery and a circular pathway that surrounded the river Derwent, and not far off a hundred acres in size.

As beautiful as it was, its size and popularity meant it was not a simple place to search for clues to find Barb, and it was even harder to block if off from the public thanks to its five separate entrances. It was also a conservation area, which brought its own problems. He could do nothing without an application— not unless there was a risk to life.

As it was a potential kidnapping case, Murray authorised two dog handlers to visit the park with Swanson, Hart, and Summer. The trio wrapped up in thick coats, hats, and scarves and stood in the courtyard of the charming tearooms, the last place Swanson had seen Barb's smile. Families and smiling couples surrounded them, enjoying their winter walks or resting in the courtyard with a hot brew. The faint smell of chips lingered in the air. Any other day he would've been all over a few chips before a walk around the park, but the smell made his stomach even more nauseous.

The two officers Murray had sent were Jean Merrick and Tom Brown. They stood next to Swanson near the exit of the courtyard. Straight on from there was a small hill that led to the path which followed the river Derwent. The pair stuck out more than the others thanks to their black vests emblazoned with POLICE as well as their radios and other gadgets. There were also the two highly trained English springer spaniels with their own black police harnesses. The eager little dogs were already looking around, and their floppy ears trailed the ground as they sniffed and strained to be let off the lead.

"Did you know this place has the largest collection of hydrangeas in Britain?" Hart asked.

"How on earth do you know that?" he asked, giving her a sideways glance.

She shrugged. "I came for a walk once and there was an open day with a guided tour for the hydrangeas."

Swanson pulled a face. "That doesn't sound like something you'd be into. Flowers aren't really you, are they?"

"I quite enjoyed it, actually," she muttered. "It was peaceful."

She crossed her arms defensively and looked down at the dogs instead with a wary eye. Hart was more of a cat lady, unlike Summer who he'd almost had to forcibly hold back from cuddling the dogs when they arrived. He and Summer could get a dog when all of this was over and Barb was back at home drinking her posh version of prosecco.

"Right. Let's go see if they find anything," Brown said,

turning to smile at Swanson. "Hopefully it's a live one!"

What a prick. He wasn't sure if Jones knew that the missing person was his aunt, but he wanted to punch him either way. Merrick didn't seem to like his comment either judging from the disgusted look she gave him. But she ignored him and focused on getting the harness off her pup. The pair ran off like little whippets with their ears bouncing up and down with each step. The dog handlers walked quickly after them, and the other three followed.

"Do you think they'll find anything?" Hart asked Swanson quietly as they walked down the short hill to the river.

"No. I think this whole thing is a windup. They're probably watching us right now and laughing their sick heads off. Why would they tell me where she is? It doesn't make any sense."

His voice raised with each word and he tried to swallow down the anger crawling around inside him as they followed the fast dogs. They ran in several directions searching for a scent. Merrick had already explained that she'd trained her pup to find the scent of decay—meaning death. Jones trained his pup for sniffing out missing people. He was most often searching for lost people in the nearby Peak District mountains and hillsides.

Swanson walked behind the dogs, striding to keep up. He followed them along the path, which curved around the river Derwent and through the park. Until one dog barked and ran off at incredible speed.

Swanson bolted after it before he even realised what was happening. Jones and Merrick followed, with the second dog running behind them excitedly. He heard Hart's footsteps behind him but pushed himself to run harder to keep up with the dog. Whether they'd found the scent of a body or a live person, he didn't know. It was impossible to tell which dog was which. The two dogs were identical to him.

The bolting dog ran right past a restaurant near the cotton mill and continued past a roaring dam. It ran so far that it passed the exit of the park before stopping in a field and barking continuously. The spot he'd stopped at was a piece of grass behind some shrubbery.

Swanson's heart beat battered his chest by the time they reached the dog. There was a lump of panic in his throat that was about to consume him. Because he knew this must be the cadaver dog.

It could smell the scent of rotting flesh.

Swanson took a few wobbly steps backwards, ending up by the entrance to the park whilst Merrick inspected the area. She bent down and looked at the ground carefully. It looked like she was digging slowly with her hand.

Swanson's feet wouldn't move any further. He couldn't move any closer to help and unable to run away like he wanted to. Hart was nowhere to be seen, neither was Summer. They probably got lost trying to catch up.

"It's loose soil. And clothing!" Merrick called as Brown approached with the second dog. She threw the dogs some treats and got on the phone. "It looks like a red coat. I'll call it in."

The spell over Swanson broke, and he ran forward. He pushed Merrick out of the way and she grunted as she fell to the ground on her back. He pulled at the red material.

It was the same shade as Aunt Barb's favourite red coat.

"Hey! What are you doing?" Jones yelled. "It needs to be done by—"

Swanson stopped listening. The blood pounding in his ears made it impossible. The coat wasn't deep in the ground. He dug it out with his hands, flinging soil everywhere. As soon as he could, he yanked the bulk from the ground.

Something heavy was wrapped inside the coat. It was too small to be Barb, but it did smell of death. He tried not to gag as he unwrapped the coat and prayed this wasn't the moment he discovered something he could never unsee. Something that would confirm her death.

But the relief hit him like a truck when he saw it was the body of a dog. He dropped it to the ground, wheezing.

"Swanson!" Hart's breathless shout reached him. "You could've messed everything up then! Come on. Let's get out of here. Now. Up. Move."

She sounded so far away yet her hands pulled at his shoulders. He allowed her to drag him unsteadily to his feet, but once he stood up the air closed in around him and he pushed her away and stumbled to the edge of the park. He roared as he propelled the heel of his boot into the nearby fence, and the sound of splintering wood rang through the park. The shards shattered around his ankle. He swallowed down the pain with a renewed sense of rage. Anonymous was going to pay for this if it was the last thing they did. With the rage running through him they'd be lucky if they made it to prison.

19

Summer

Summer was breathless by the time she reached the second park. Joshua's school had called just as one of the adorable little spaniels ran off barking, and she had no idea if it was the one who sniffed out live things or not. The school rarely called unless he was ill and needed to be picked up. Although this time it was to say poor Joshua had a bit of a fall and bumped his head but he seemed fine.

But before she even got to the gate, she could see that Swanson wasn't there. Hart stared glumly at a broken fence with her hands on her hips. Her head shot up as she heard Summer call her name.

"What happened to you?" she yelled across the fence.

"The school rang when I started to run," Summer replied, still breathing heavily as she approached the small wooden gate. "I couldn't keep up and talk."

Hart looked her up and down. "You need to get that cheap gym membership through work and get your cardio on."

Summer grinned as she closed the little gate behind her and stood next to Hart. The hole in the fence was pretty big.

Someone had hit it hard.

"Where is he?" she asked Hart.

"Well, he did that"—she pointed at the fence—"and then ran off. So your guess is as good as mine."

"Why did he hurt the fence?"

"You can't *hurt* a fence, Summer. It isn't human." She sighed heavily. "The dog found something buried over there, where Merrick and Jones are taking pictures."

Summer turned to stare at the two dog handlers. They looked mightily pissed off about something.

"They don't look as happy as they did earlier. What are they so upset about?"

"Swanson kind of nearly messed everything up."

"Of course he did. I'm worried about him. What did he do?"

"The cadaver dog was barking at something on the ground and Merrick dug down a little and found a red coat, which is the same shade as Barb's favourite winter coat according to her missing persons report."

"Ah, I see." She had a sinking feeling about Hart's next words.

"Merrick tried to call it in officially. But Swanson saw it and pushed Merrick to the ground to get her out of the way."

Summer gasped and looked over at Merrick again. She seemed fine, though she was rubbing her shoulder a little. Pushing a woman was the sort of thing Swanson was highly against. Unless he needed to arrest them, anyway.

"She's okay, and I've told her it's his aunt so she won't lodge a complaint or anything. Merrick has always been sound."

"He's lucky, though," Summer mumbled. "Was it really Barb's coat?"

"Yes. It was her coat but not her body."

"Come again?"

"The sick bastard wrapped a dead dog in Barb's coat to fuck with Swanson."

Summer puffed her cheeks and let out a long, slow breath. "So it was then he kicked the fence?"

"Yes."

"Right. Well, surely we need to find him before he does any more damage."

"You won't find him for a while. He needs to lick his wounds alone first," Hart replied.

Summer nodded. For the first time, she felt a stab of jealousy at how well Hart knew him. Of course Swanson would need alone time first.

She should've known that herself.

"You may as well get off now, Summer." Hart finally turned away from the shattered fence to face her. "Merrick is going to bag up the coat for forensics and I'm going to find out about the CCTV around here. I'm guessing they chose this park instead of Darley Abbey because it's quieter with no surrounding CCTV. I don't think we'll have much luck."

"Sure. I'll see you later. Let me know if you find anything out. Swanson gets tunnel vision and forgets to tell me."

"Will do."

Summer moved to walk away but stopped and turned back to face Hart. "I'm worried about him."

Hart wore a grim expression. She nodded in agreement. "Same. Let's face the facts. Poor Barb is probably not alive. He seems to be adamant that she is. At this rate he'll mess up the investigation so whoever has hurt her won't get sent down. He's acting erratic. I can't say I would act any differently, but we really need to monitor him. Murray isn't happy that his idiot cousin Ger already made a formal complaint about him, and when I went to see Dotty Foster, she wasn't too happy about his conduct either."

"What did she say?"

"Something about how she shouldn't have to be told that her sister is dead by a strange man on his own. She seems wound up too tightly. She also accused him of aggressively asking her questions to help straight after telling her Mandy Harris is dead."

"Nothing had even happened to Barb at that point, though," Summer replied.

"Nope. Like I said, I think she's just highly strung. Just be there quietly for him for now, Summer. He will need you when we confirm her death at some point."

Summer nodded and walked through the little exit gate. She waved bye to Hart as she trudged back through the field surrounding the park. Two hundred feet away she spotted someone crouching down near a thick tree trunk.

She froze. There was something about that figure that was familiar. They weren't looking at her; they were looking at their shoes. It looked like they were tying up a lace or something. Just like that person outside the cafe. Then it hit her.

They were wearing the same coat.

"Hart!" Summer yelled without taking her eyes off the person. She waved at Hart to come to her.

But the person's head shot up when she shouted, and they caught her staring right at them. She couldn't see their face, and time froze for a brief second. Her mouth became so dry it was hard to breathe and her legs were suddenly numb. The person stood slowly, deliberately keeping their head down. They took a step forward, and for a moment she thought they were going to charge at her.

Her life was about to be over, and she'd frozen to the spot.

But something behind Summer made the person's head turn, and they suddenly bolted in the other direction instead.

"There! Hart, there!" Summer screamed and pointed in the direction they'd run. "That was the person who snapped a picture of me in the cafe! I know it."

Summer assumed Hart would call for backup, but she was after them herself in a shot. One of the dog handlers ran off after her. The feeling slowly returned to Summer's legs just as the other dog handler reached her.

"Are you okay? You look very pale. Come and sit down." Merrick put her arm through Summer's and led her back to the park.

"That person just gave me the most horrible feeling."

"Is that why you sent Hart after them? You think they took this missing lady?"

"All I know is they were watching me outside a cafe before, and now they're here watching again. They were probably the one who took the picture."

"What picture? Sit down."

Summer realised Merrick had walked her all the way back to the park and was now pointing at a wooden bench.

"Thanks. Just some picture of me in a cafe. It isn't important, really."

"Here." Merrick handed her a bottle of water from nowhere. "This will help."

Summer took the bottle and drank gratefully. The dizziness eased as the water filled her body. She'd never felt that way when she looked at anyone before. A feeling overcame her as if her whole body had been drained and she would never move freely again.

"The pup will help too." Merrick picked up one of the spaniels and placed them on the bench next to Summer.

The other dog had run off with Jones. The spaniel instantly started sniffing around the bench and then around Summer. She smiled as she stroked the warm, floppy ears gently. The dog flipped onto their back and she stroked its soft belly.

"It really does help," she muttered.

Her phone buzzed from her pocket and tickled her leg. She pulled it out quickly in case it was Swanson or the school ringing again. But it was Hart.

"We lost them." She breathed heavily down the phone. "They were too fast."

Summer's heart sank. "Okay. What now?"

"Me, CCTV. You go home and stay safe. I'll get the car now and pick you up from there. Call Swanson, please. Tell him what happened if you can. I reckon he's more likely to answer your call than mine."

Summer hung up and cuddled the soft pup a little tighter. The flat was the same place the last stalker had broken in and tried to stab her. The cottage should be home by now but yet here she was again. Merrick walked off to greet some forensics people, and the dog scrambled off Summer's lap to follow her.

Feeling even more alone, she tried to call Swanson. As usual, he didn't answer. She sighed and threw the phone in her bag. He was such a difficult person to be there for. For now, it was just her to look after Joshua again, and maybe that's the way it would always be.

20

Swanson

S wanson refreshed his phone again. Still no new messages. Nothing from the team regarding the anonymous number. Nothing from Hart about Dotty Foster. Summer had called, but he had no head space to talk to her. She'd understand.

Aunt Barb dominated his thoughts. Her smile and laughter consumed his sleep. The guilt that she might be starving somewhere in darkness, shivering and scared, was gnawing at his veins as if tiny bugs had invaded his body.

Since the incident with the dead dog in the park, he'd spent more than two hours searching Darley Abbey for any clues. There was something he was missing. An obvious clue lay somewhere right in front of him, but try as he might, it wouldn't come to him. He'd even broken into what looked like an abandoned warehouse, only to find an overly friendly homeless man who offered him a can of beer.

A press release had aired on the news at lunchtime, and it had caused a huge upset in the community she lived in. Barb was a well-known and much loved figure to her neighbours.

She'd lived there for a long time and knew everyone pretty well. Thanks to her natural generosity, she'd helped many of them out once or twice with different things. So a couple crowds of people from the area had gathered together to go out looking for her. But they may as well have not bothered. There was no sign of her anywhere and there was a higher likelihood of them accidentally trashing evidence in Swanson's opinion.

Ger was with one group. It looked like he was basking in the attention. How poor Barb ended up with two sons like that was beyond Swanson. She was too good for either of them.

He'd returned to Barb's office to keep away from Ger and his helpers and stared at a map of the town instead. He shivered and pulled his coat around him. The tips of his fingers and toes were numb from being out in the cold for so long. There'd been no heating in the house since Barb disappeared. She didn't like having it on a schedule because it was a big house and it cost too much.

But if she returned home at that moment, she'd be freezing. So he walked into the kitchen and opened up the corner cupboard, which housed the boiler. He flicked on the heating and it fired up nicely. The noise made the empty house seem warmer already. Like it was just waiting for her to walk in the door and confirm she'd kicked some idiot's ass and needed a glass of whiskey.

He returned to the office and took a seat at the desk. It felt strange sitting in Barb's chair, but his body ached and his brain was so tired. He rested his head in his hands, squeezed his eyes closed, and let the darkness invade him. There must be something he was missing. Some silly clue or random piece of evidence that would help him find her. It had been forty-eight hours since she was called in missing. If he relaxed and cleared his overtired mind, it could come to light.

Then the darkness took over completely, and before he knew it, the sun was seeping in through the white blinds of the east-facing window in the office. The desk felt hard against his cheek. He dragged his head up off the desk and groaned, confused by the light. The digital clock perched precariously on the edge of the desk ticked over to 8:00 a.m.

Shit.

The chair fell to the ground as he jumped up at the realisation he'd slept all night on the damn desk. The painful crick in the base of his neck let him know his body had barely moved the whole time; and his head ached even worse than it had the previous night.

He picked up the chair and threw it back into place underneath the desk. The kitchen was down the hall, but dizziness hit him as he tried to make his way there. Every inch of his body cried out for rehydration. He eventually made it to the kitchen sink and grabbed a glass from the drainage board. He was about to put water in it when a thought hit him.

Aunt Barb never left glasses on the drainage board.

He stared at the glass in his shaky hand then dropped it back down. Unless it belonged to one of the forensics people, which would be a huge offence as a contamination of a crime scene, it could have DNA of whoever was in the house with Barb.

But the pain in his head was too bad to think straight. He grabbed a fresh glass from the cupboard and filled it with water. His body was so dehydrated he could feel the water running through his veins. Once he'd downed it, he drank another just as quick.

It wasn't until the water was flowing through him he woke up and realised where he was. In *Aunt Barb's* kitchen. His stomach dropped as he remembered it was real. She was missing. It wasn't just a nightmare.

Feeling less shaky, he examined the glass again. He couldn't see anything on it, but if there was any chance at all that there was a clue here, it needed to be checked out. He rummaged in the drawers that surrounded Barb's country-style kitchen, eventually finding some sandwich bags in one drawer to wrap up the glass.

He crossed the hall to the office to gather his things before heading back to the station with the glass. Then he could get out around Darley Abbey looking for her again. He'd left his phone on the desk, and as he approached, he saw it flashing.

He picked it up to check the notifications, and his jaw clenched as he saw it was another text message from the anonymous asshole. This time they'd only sent two words.

Dig Deeper.

21

Swanson

Swanson also had five missed calls from Murray, Hart, and Summer. Plus another from Simone Jones, a victim he'd worked with last year. He cleared them all. None of that mattered to him. The new text mattered. He called Hart, though. Even after everything that had happened between them in the past couple days, she was the one who would help him.

"Yes, stranger?" she barked down the phone.

Normally her sarcasm would make him smile, but that felt so wrong when Barb was gone.

"Dig deeper," he said, unable to get more words out to explain what he was referring to. Either lack of sleep or lack of water had really made his brain wonky.

"I'm sorry what? Have you been drink—"

"Dig deeper," he said again. His fists clenched. He took another breath to steady his thoughts.

"Dig bloody where?" she replied in a huff. "What are you on about?"

"That's what I'm asking you. I got another text from that

asshole. All it says is 'dig deeper'. What do you think it means?"

"Dig deeper into what? Like is there a clue to dig deeper into metaphorically or does it mean physically dig deeper somewhere?"

"How should I know?" he snapped. "I haven't slept in days and need a fuck ton of water to get rehydrated again."

"Where are you?" she asked. "Summer couldn't find you after the search last night. She said you weren't at home and didn't call her back. You made us both worry, you idiot."

Again the guilt crawled further into his veins like little maggots worming their way around under his skin. "I'm sorry. I was out most of the night looking."

"Looking for what?"

"I don't know! Just looking. For clues or places or anything, really."

Hart sighed heavily. "Just call Summer or something for god's sake. She's out of her mind with worry about you. We want to help, you know."

A faint, familiar voice came from Hart's background. "Is that Swanson?"

"Who the hell is that?" he asked, but as soon as the question left his lips he realised. "Is that Murray? Are you with her?"

"No one. Never mind who it is. Text me where you are and I'll meet you."

He could almost hear her cheeks turning pink from embarrassment as she hung up, and he had to allow himself a small smile. At least someone he cared for was happy. He texted her to meet him near the park where they'd found the dead dog, and then grabbed his hat, coat, and gloves. He picked up the bag containing the glass too and walked outside to place it in the boot of his car. The temperature outside had dropped so much that the frost had almost frozen the boot shut.

He climbed into the freezing car and turned on the heat, getting frustrated as he waited for the windshield to defrost. The park was only around the corner from Barb's, but he felt the need to bring the car. He wanted a quick way of getting anywhere if he got a hint where Barb was being kept. It briefly crossed his mind that if she was outside, this cold weather would kill her off. But he pushed the thought away.

He finally made it to the park fifteen minutes after leaving the house, and to his surprise Hart was already waiting for him. She approached the car as he pulled up. She was well wrapped up in a dark, knee-length winter coat.

"You were quick," he said. "It normally takes at least twenty minutes from yours."

"I drove quickly. I told Murray about the most recent text you received. She's sending some people out here to the park to help look for clues. We have nothing back from the coat yet, but she requested it's looked at urgently."

"You mean she was with you when I told you. You were at her house, weren't you?"

She folded her arms across her chest. "Let's focus on Barb, shall we?"

"I'm focused on nothing else," he replied. "But it's okay to talk about Murray. I know her place is closer to ten minutes from here."

"Is it now?" Her face was stony as she turned to him. "You might accuse me of being a traitor again."

"I would never do that." He managed a grin.

Hart tutted and tried to keep a straight face, but it resulted in a snort of laughter. "You're unbelievable. And you're in desperate need of an iron."

She turned away from him, shaking her head. Her shiny bob shook gently.

"I have a glass to pass on to forensics too."

"A glass?"

"Yes. It was on the drainage board."

She raised an eyebrow. "What makes you think it isn't Barb's?"

"She never leaves glasses on the drainage board. It's uncouth."

"If you say so. Anything is worth a shot. Now, why are you putting off talking about this text? Show it to me."

An icy coldness creeped into his veins. This text was different. Short and sweet. There was only one point to it: to scare him. Like all the texts, really. But he couldn't keep this one.

"I deleted it," he confessed.

He'd learned more about this anonymous person since their first text. The same one Hart thought was a poor joke or some idiot chancer. Those two words had zapped all hope from his soul. Because he now knew they were evil enough to send him on a goose chase for his aunt, and so they were definitely evil enough to hurt Barb.

"Why the hell would you do that?"

He shrugged. "The others disappeared anyway. How does that even happen?"

"The sender recalled them somehow, I guess. Deleting it sooner will not make it go away, Swanson," she said in a more gentle tone.

He hated that tone. It didn't suit her. Her sarcastic bitch demeanour was much preferable to him.

"Don't get soft on me, Hart. What do you think it meant, anyway?"

"It's one of two things. Dig deeper into the clues we have. Such as the people we've interviewed and things we've found."

"Or?"

"Or dig deeper physically."

His stomach clenched. Could Aunt Barb really be in that hole? It made little sense. She was always so bright and elegant, the life and soul of any party. The one constant person throughout his life who he could rely on. She would do what was best for him even when it pissed him off.

They wandered back down to the park to meet the crew Murray had ordered. It didn't take long for them to arrive. They had blocked the site of the coat discovery off to the public already following yesterday's find. A team had stayed for a bit to hunt for clues, but there was no scene guard appointed to watch the place afterwards. No officers could be spared for that unless they found a human body.

"I just got a text about the coat," Hart said as they walked over to the site with a fresh crew of officers.

"What about it?" he asked.

"They found DNA that didn't match Barb's. They're going to look into it but the culprit might not be as clever as they think if they've left us a trail."

He nearly smiled. The thought of catching the person behind her disappearance was amazing, but it wasn't quite enough. It wasn't enough to remove the dread he felt at the possibility of finding her dead. Everything else seemed so futile and unimportant in comparison to finding her alive. Hell, he'd let them go if it meant her being alive.

"I need to go," he said.

"What? I thought that news would cheer you up. You're the one who dragged us all here. Where are you going?"

"I'll be back soon. Text me when you have an update."

He walked away in no specific direction. His feet found the path at Darley Abbey and continued on to the park. He turned off his phone and shoved it back into his pocket. It was peaceful walking by the river and listening to the sounds of the water rippling gently. It was just the kind of walk Barb would love.

He studied the long branches of the trees that towered above him along each path. He'd never really noticed the variety before. The park had oaks, sycamores, maples, cedars, plus more he didn't recognise. People passed him in their droves. Groups of friends, families, and elderly couples clinging to each other.

He walked past a kids' park, where the noise of them playing almost made him stop. A small boy younger than Joshua ran past him to enter the play park, his nose bright red from the frosty morning. They were all babies, with the school-aged kids being stuck inside learning for a while yet.

He strolled so slowly that it took two hours for him to find the same opening he'd used to enter the park. The field they were digging up was beyond, around the corner from the houses. Summer was at the entrance. She took him by surprise and for a moment he wondered if he was imagining her.

Her hair was windswept, and her pale skin was blotchy from the cold. He wanted nothing more than to reach out to her and go for a walk. They should just keep walking and forget anything else that was happening.

She looked straight at him, and stood calmly and waited for him to reach her. She didn't smile as he approached. Instead, she held out her hand. He took it automatically, and she squeezed it hard. He knew what she was going to say before she even opened her mouth.

"Hart called me. I'm so sorry, babe. They've found her," she said.

He closed his eyes to ward off the dizziness that threatened to make him fall over and reached out to hold on to the post next to Summer.

"Where is she?" he asked, though his throat was thick.

"Exactly where you said she was. In the same hole as they had buried the poor dog. The dog was a red herring. Don't go up there, please. Stay here with me."

He tried to reply but his chest tightened. He let go of her hand and brought his own palm to his chest, wheezing as he tried to suck in more air.

"Swanson, breathe." Summer's soft voice reached him, but his breath was gone. He felt his body fall against something cold and hard. The fence? Maybe it was the ground. It was over. That was it. He'd failed the one person who had never failed him. The one who was always there for him no matter what. Someone had taken her from him right under his nose. And now that someone had to pay.

22

Summer

Summer forced the trolley unwillingly around the supermarket. It had been twenty-four hours since she'd seen Swanson. He'd ignored all of her texts and calls completely. Which would be fine *if* she knew he was okay. He hadn't replied to Hart, either. The worry was eating away at her brain. She should swing by the cottage to check on him. Dropping off some food might be a good idea. He was a mess last time she'd seen him.

A weird feeling overcame her, and she turned around, expecting someone she knew to be behind her. But no one was there. Christ. The paranoia was real. The threatening feeling had lurked in the back of her mind since someone had lured her to the cafe under the false pretence of meeting Aarron. That same person had murdered poor Barb and buried her heartlessly in a public park. They'd even killed a dog and taunted Swanson. It was clearly a very disturbed and dangerous individual they were dealing with.

As she reached the frozen aisle, she passed a familiar looking, pale brunette. The woman turned to her and smiled. She looked friendly enough, but Summer couldn't place her face at all.

"Hi, Summer," the woman said.

Summer recoiled and took a step back.

"Er, hi," she replied. "Sorry, I'm not sure where we know each other from."

"I'm Simone Jones. I'm sort of a . . . friend of Alex's."

None of Swanson's friends called him Alex that Summer knew of. Only his Aunt Barb called him that. Or used to.

"How do you know Alex?" she asked, not minding the fact that her voice came out full of suspicion. Let the woman know she was suspicious.

"I was attacked last year and he helped me out. I'm actually an online content creator now. I used to be a journalist—"

"No," Summer interrupted as the familiarity finally clicked. Simone was someone who Swanson had worked with the previous year. Summer remembered a story about her in the paper.

"Sorry?" A look of puzzlement crossed Simone's face.

"I know what you're going to ask. The answer is no. I have no information for you." Summer pushed the trolley in the opposite direction and tried to walk away.

"Please, Summer. I know it's hard to trust an ex-journalist, but I just want to help Alex like he helped me before. I want to find out the truth for him about who killed his aunt, but no one can reach him."

Summer let go of the trolley and whipped around to face Simone.

"How do you know that? No one should know that until tonight's press release. And how do you even know my name for that matter?"

She shrugged. "I still have my sources from being a journalist."

"Well, tell your sources to go fuck themselves," Summer spat. She shoved the trolley away from her and stormed past Simone.

Fucking journalists and their stupid sources getting off on gossiping about Swanson's pain and poor Barb's death. How dare they?

She kept going all the way through the shop and out of the store. She didn't stop until she reached the car parked in the furthest corner of the car park—a habit she'd taken from Swanson. Only then did she stop and soak in the fresh air to calm her temper. But still she felt Simone's eyes on her.

She whipped around and sure enough, Simone had followed her. She stood a few feet away and looked as calm as anything whilst Summer's hands trembled with rage.

"Why the hell did you follow me?" she yelled.

"I really do want to help because Alex helped me." Simone raised her hands, palms forward. She held something in between her right thumb and forefinger. "Here's my card with my phone number just in case you change your mind."

"Why don't you speak to him yourself?" Summer asked irritably, though her temper was calming down now that she was outside. It was hard to be angry in minus a thousand degrees.

"If he doesn't answer your calls then what makes you think he would answer mine?" Simone asked. She stepped forward slowly and placed the card on Summer's car bonnet. "You can ask him who I am, though."

"Fine." Summer rolled her eyes and grabbed the card from the bonnet before yanking the driver's door open. "Just leave me alone now."

"Okay. Speak to you soon."

Summer felt her temper flare again at Simone's cocky words. She spun around to say something else, but the woman was already quite a few feet away across the car park.

"Hey!" Summer yelled, too annoyed to care about the other shoppers now staring at her like she was out of her mind. "How did you know he isn't answering the phone to me?"

"I didn't! But you're clearly upset about something," Simone called back without turning around.

Summer felt her cheeks turning pink. *What an absolute cow.* She got into the car and threw the card, and it floated weakly down to the passenger side floor, which ended up annoying her even more. Fuck Swanson ignoring her calls. She shoved her seat belt into place and jammed the car into gear. The asshole was getting support whether or not he threw it back in her face.

23

Swanson

The wooden frame of the sofa dug into Swanson's head as he shifted his position. The cushioning around the frame was old, and starting to weaken. Daylight fell on his face and pulled him rudely from the sleep he desperately wanted to get back to. He groaned at the painful pulse running through his head caused by copious amounts of Aunt Barb's favourite whiskey. Without opening his eyes, he reached out to feel for the bottle of water he usually left on the floor. But it was gone.

He forced himself up and off the sofa, stumbling to the kitchen for hydration to numb the ache. His whole body hurt when he got up. It wasn't until he finished his glass of water that the previous day's events came crashing back to him. Summer's face as she told him they'd found Barb's body would haunt him for a long time. He'd had to leave because he couldn't even look at her.

A knock at the door barely registered to his brain. He glanced over at the tilted wooden door, but screw whoever was knocking. He downed another glass of water and placed it into the sink. The numbness he'd felt upon waking was wearing off, replaced with a heaviness in his heart that only more whiskey was going to medicate. The knocking at the door came again, louder this time. He cursed and glared at the door but still didn't move to answer it. After a few seconds they banged so hard that the door shook, followed by the letterbox being pushed open.

"Swanson, let me in right now or I will knock this damn door down!" Summer yelled through the gap.

Panic flooded him. "What the hell? Are you okay?" he called as he finally lumbered through the living room. Which was hard work when his body was still as stiff as a board.

He made it across and threw open the front door. A furious Summer pushed past him. Her cheeks were pinker than he'd ever seen. She didn't even look at him. She glared at the mess on his living room floor. A mess that he'd only just noticed. He looked away from it, embarrassed.

"Is someone chasing you?" He craned his neck to get a better view of the street, but it was empty. The neighbour's orange cat was the only thing he could see. She sat next to his car licking her paws. An icy breeze tickled his bare arms, and he shivered.

"What? No. Of course not. What the hell is going on in here? You look like someone has robbed you."

"Why are you banging on my door like someone is about to kill you?" he asked as he quickly closed the door.

"I'm here for you. You didn't answer any of my calls. Or Hart's. We've been worried."

"I'm fine," he snapped as he lurched over to the sofa to sit down again. His head spun from moving around too quickly.

"Un huh. You look great. Get a shower. I'll tidy up here."

He glared up at her like a stubborn child, and she glared right back at him.

"Go now or god help me I will get the hose and wash you down right here, Alex Swanson. I am a mother. Do not mess with me."

She placed one hand on her hip, and a ripple of laughter built up in his chest at the idea of her hosing him down in the living room. He tried to swallow it back down, but his lips twitched and it ended up releasing in a snort of laughter that he couldn't stop or control. He laughed until his side ached and tears ran down his cheeks whilst Summer stared at him.

"Okay. Now I'm completely lost," she said once he'd stopped wheezing. "Why have you gone from looking at me like you want to kill me to laughing at me?"

"You just did exactly what Aunt Barb would have done," he replied, still grinning. It was nice to be reminded of her.

"Oh," Summer shifted uncomfortably as if suddenly unsure how to stand. "Well, she sounded great, so I'll take that as a compliment, I guess."

"It is a compliment." Swanson stood and stretched out the crick in his neck again. It hadn't gone away since falling asleep on Barb's desk. He passed Summer awkwardly to get to the stairs, but when he paused as he started to climb them, she was still staring at him. Her face was hard set, but her eyes were full of worry. He felt bad for not at least texting her to say he was okay. But that would've been a lie, anyway. He wasn't okay. But things were better now that she was here.

"Thanks," he said.

Her lips parted as if she was going to say something, but she closed them and waved him up the stairs. She turned around and started picking up rubbish from the floor, and he carried on up the stairs to the bathroom. Just turning on the shower felt like a colossal waste of his efforts, but he flicked it on regardless and forced himself to stand under the hot water.

By the time he returned downstairs twenty minutes later, the place looked much nicer. Summer had kept her word and tidied up. There were no longer any empty bottles of alcohol strewn across the floor or leftover takeaway. It smelled much nicer too. So did he in a fresh suit. The shower felt good. It didn't take away the pain in his chest like the whiskey did, mind. Summer appeared in the kitchen doorway.

"It looks great in here," he said.

"You look better too. I'm going to make bacon sandwiches. Sit down."

Summer pointed towards the kitchen table, and he didn't have the energy to argue. Or the heart to tell her he wasn't hungry. So he did as he was told. She plonked a glass of water in front of him and busied herself with a frying pan while he watched.

Soon the smell of sizzling bacon rashers filled the kitchen, and his stomach growled. He had a sudden urge to tell Summer to get her things from her flat. If this was what her moving in would be like, then he could easily get used to it. And although the aching numbness from losing Barb was still there, her presence did actually ease it. It was just missing the eight-year-old whirlwind and his many police-related questions.

"Where's Joshua?" he asked.

"School." She turned to grab the loaf of farmhouse bread from the cupboard behind him but stopped when she spotted his blank look. "It's Wednesday afternoon, babe."

"Right. Yes. I knew that," he lied.

So they found Aunt Barb on a Tuesday. He wondered what day she died. How long had she been in that awful hole? Alone in the cold and waiting for him to rescue her. His stomach clenched. Suddenly he didn't want a bacon sandwich.

"Why are you wearing a suit? You're not going to work. Murray won't let you in."

He shrugged. "Just out of habit. It's not like I'm ill."

"Of course you are. If mental illness was treated more like physical illness and people could rest guilt-free when feeling down, we'd all be a lot happier and less stressed."

"I'm not ill mentally or physically!"

"Don't be stupid. You're bereaved, and this is exactly what I'm talking about."

"Do you know anything more about what happened? Has Hart said anything?"

She'd grabbed the bread by now and was busy buttering four slices. She'd visited so many times that she moved around the kitchen as if she already lived there.

"Summer? Please tell me," he asked gently. "I need to know. I know it won't be nice but it's probably no worse than what's been going through my mind."

"It's fine. I'll tell you what I know. Let me just finish doing this. I had a journalist asking me questions in the supermarket earlier." She grabbed the bottle of brown sauce and squirted it on the bread.

"Which newspaper were they from?"

The flare of anger he would usually feel at the thought of journalists hounding Summer whilst shopping didn't appear. His emotions weren't working properly.

"Well, she said she was an *ex*-journalist to be specific. Now she has some sort of online news channel on social media." Summer turned and placed a tower of bacon sandwiches in front of him. His stomach grumbled and his appetite reappeared big time.

"Simone Jones?" he asked, remembering the missed call he had from her yesterday. He took a big bite of the first sandwich and closed his eyes for a second to savour the taste. "This is so good. Thank you."

"You're welcome, and yes. She said you helped her with something and you trust her?" Summer asked tentatively.

"It was a case a while back. She was attacked outside her home. I don't know her other than that. She seemed okay, but I don't trust or mistrust her. What did you tell her about the case?"

"Nothing! I wasn't about to spill it all to some ex-journalist. I was a bit rude to her, actually. Possibly unnecessarily so. She accosted me when I was shopping, and I just got annoyed at her for wanting likes on social media for your pain."

"That doesn't surprise me. Simone's very thorough from what I've seen. She called me yesterday, but I haven't given her anything. She's the kind of woman who never gives up, though." He went for another bite of sandwich but froze before it got to his lips. "*She* never gives up."

"Yes, you said that already."

"*She*, Summer. Aunt Barb must have gone with a woman. There's no sign of a struggle. Aunt Barb let someone in before they most likely bonked her on the head to cause that trail of blood patches. She trusted someone enough to let them in, and she wouldn't have trusted a man. She has a thing about men just like she had a thing about leaving dirty glasses on the drainage board. She *had* a thing about them. Anonymous is probably a woman too. A nasty, vindictive one. I'm sure of it."

"I like your theory. There's no evidence, but it wouldn't surprise me if this was the work of a woman."

"Tell me about her death, Summer."

Summer sighed heavily and reached out to squeeze his hand. "She had a nasty bang to the head and someone stabbed her at least once. That's all we know until the postmortem."

"That's weirdly close, personal, and violent for a woman but not too uncommon," he replied.

Summer let go of his hand and raised her eyebrows. "And that was a weirdly clinical reaction to finding out how your aunt died."

"I'm okay, Summer. Promise. I feel so much better after a shower and food." He took another huge bite of the sandwich, feeling more like himself with each bit of food.

"Good," she replied. "I'm supposed to be getting Joshua soon. Are you going to be okay if I go?"

"Yes. I'm fine. Off you go. Call me later."

He shovelled the last bite of sandwich into his mouth as she collected her things and then walked her through the living room to the front door. The light was already low outside. It would be dark pretty soon.

"You better answer," she said as she stepped out onto the drive.

"I will. I'm sorry I made you worry." He leaned over the threshold to kiss her softly.

"Make sure you rest up and call me if you need anything."

She walked away, and he forced a calm look as he waved goodbye. But after she drove off, he closed the door, pushed his feet into black shoes, and grabbed a warm, quilted overcoat. The same one Hart had brought him the previous Christmas because she said looking at him made her cold.

Excitement tingled through him, covering up the solid ball of grief in his chest now that he knew what he had to do. He stepped outside and lit up a cigarette. Then he grabbed his phone and called the only person he knew who would help him without bleating on about grief and rest.

"Alex? Is that you?" Simone Jones answered on the third ring. Her voice was calm and serious. Just like he remembered her.

"Yes. I need your help."

"Happy to. I heard about your aunt. I'm so sorry."

He hoped she was as sincere as she sounded. "Do you still have your contacts at the station?"

"Yes. What do you need?"

"First, I need to know all about Mandy Harris."

"She was quite boring and retired. Before that she was a teacher at a school for kids with special behavioural needs—"

"What kind of needs?" he interrupted.

"Naughty kids. Disruptive kids. Foster kids. Some had criminal records and the like. She retired last year. She'd never been in any trouble legally. No kids herself and never been married. She's lived with her sister for years. She was polite to her neighbours but never talked much and didn't seem to have many friends outside of her sister."

"Thanks. That helps a lot. I also need to know how a social worker affords a property worth over one million pounds." Summer had told him after their visit that it was a vast house and she couldn't see how a social worker living alone could afford it.

"Send me a name and an address with any background."

He hung up from Simone and stubbed out the cigarette. A plan to find out who had murdered Barb had already formed in his mind, and it started with a visit to Nadene Andersson.

24

Swanson

Swanson couldn't wait for Simone to get back to him. There was no time, and it wasn't like Andersson lived close by. Simone was good. Maybe she'd have an answer for him by the time he reached her house.

He flew down the motorway and gathered his thoughts as he went. He did not know what Andersson was guilty of or if she was involved in anything related to Barb. But he would fully investigate each one of these fuckers until he knew everything from how they were born to their deepest fears. He'd leave nothing untouched. Nadene Andersson. Billy Bailey. Dotty Foster. Mandy Harris. Even Ben Jackson, the so-called friendly ex-police officer.

Before long Swanson barrelled down the narrow country road that led to Nadene Andersson's period home. Even with the warning from Summer, the sheer grandiosity of the building shocked him. A whistle escaped through his teeth when he pulled up on the tarmacked driveway. This certainly had cost someone a pretty penny.

He'd imagined the building to be inherited from her family

like most grand buildings, but this wasn't run down like a lot of them. It's all right to inherit something if you can afford the repairs; otherwise, it's nothing more than a dilapidated building. But this was so well kept it had definitely cost a lot of money over recent years.

He remembered how Summer retold of Hart losing her temper with Andersson during their visit here together. He'd struggled to imagine it when he thought of how well Hart could usually keep control of her emotions in work. But it made far more sense when he looked up at her home.

Knowing that this woman, the same person who brought kids to people like Dorothy Tilly, could live in such luxury was pretty infuriating. She'd never paid for her crimes—accidental or not. And it's not like most social workers were in it for the paltry money. It certainly wouldn't have paid to upkeep this place. There were many other much more lucrative career options if that's what interested her.

So if she didn't care about the children she was supposed to look after *and* she did not need the money judging from this house, which was her listed address at the time she brought Charlie Marsh to live with Dorothy Tilly, then what made her become a social worker?

He pulled himself out of the car. Adrenaline pumped through his veins and woke up his numb backside. Somewhere underneath that was a little voice telling him how stupid this was. He shouldn't be visiting Andersson. He was too close to it all. It was clearly a bad idea. He'd have stopped Hart in this situation.

But the fury simmering through his entire being was stronger than anything. Anonymous wasn't playing fair. If Swanson hadn't played fair, then Aunt Barb would still be alive. All he could do now was find the prick before they hurt anyone else.

He knocked on the front door a little louder than he meant to. He pulled a fake smile as best he could manage. It was silent in the house for a long few seconds. But eventually there was a shuffling noise behind the door and a shadow through the thick glass panel.

"Who is it?" called a nervous, female voice.

"It's the police, ma'am. I'm here to discuss what happened with our officer the other day and to apologise on her behalf," he lied easily.

He heard the lock click, and the door opened up to reveal a younger looking woman than he'd expected. She had fancy, thin-framed glasses, and she wore an expensive-looking blouse over soft jeans. She'd pulled her severely dark hair back into a ponytail.

"I'm surprised it took you so long to visit!" Her eyes flashed with anger and she pulled her arms across her chest. "She was awful to me. She treated me very unfairly."

Her face didn't move as she spoke. It was strange to see, and he tried hard not to stare at the smoothness of her forehead as she complained.

"I understand it was very shocking. There was a witness, and she has admitted to verbal assault. I wanted to chat with you about what happened and get a statement. Can I come in, please?"

"Of course."

He stepped inside, feeling like he had to be gentle not to crack the Victorian tiles that lined the floor. They walked past a weird-looking rocking horse thing and he narrowed his shoulders to not knock any plates off the wall when they passed dark oak stairs. She kept her arms folded as she led him through a surprisingly modern kitchen and straight into another room with a huge, oak dining table.

"Please, sit." She finally uncrossed her arms and waved towards the cream chairs that surrounded the table. She fiddled with a thin, golden locket around her neck with her other hand.

"No thank you."

She glanced at him in surprise, and he smiled widely at her and continued talking.

"Now I know what I've been told by our officer. If you can please start by explaining to me what happened in your own words."

"There were two of them, actually. Lucky for me there was the other young one. The pretty one. She pulled my aggressor away. Vile woman she was. I dread to think what might have happened otherwise." She shuddered and walked back into the kitchen. "Would you like some tea?"

He stepped into the kitchen to join her, though she flicked on the kettle without waiting for his response.

"I don't drink tea, thanks. Why did they come to visit you in the first place?" he asked.

"They wanted to talk about an old case. God knows why. I used to be a social worker, you see."

"Social workers can't afford houses like this." His voice hardened, and she turned to face him.

His fury was getting harder to push down. The more he looked at her, the more his anger brewed. She looked a lot more wary suddenly, but he forced himself to continue smiling as she spoke.

"It's so beautiful. It must cost a bomb to keep looking so pretty."

"I inherited the house." She leaned back on the counter while the kettle boiled behind her. It occurred to him she could easily throw the kettle of boiled water at him. If indeed she was dangerous and he pushed her too far.

"Ah, I see." He nodded politely. "So what was the case they wanted to speak to you about?"

She drew her eyebrows together, looking at him suspiciously. "Why does that matter?"

"I intend to make a full report." He shook his notebook in the air, not that he'd made any notes yet.

"What did you say your name was?" she asked.

"I don't believe I said my name," he replied. He hadn't planned a name, but he said the first made up one that came to mind. "It's Dan Merrick."

"Do you have your ID to confirm?" she asked. "I really should have asked when you were at the door, but I've been under a lot of stress since she attacked me."

"Of course. It's in the car."

"Are you sure you're not . . ." She stopped talking and glanced out the kitchen window as if paranoid that someone was watching her.

"Not what?" he pressed.

She sighed loudly and shook her head. "Nothing. You wouldn't tell me if you were," she muttered.

His eyes flickered down to her blouse. It was white and sheer on the arms, and as she moved her arm to grab a mug from the cupboard for her tea, he could see a purple mark on her left arm. It was on the inside of her forearm, not far above her wrist. Just where Marsh's tattoo would've been.

"Ms Andersson, I have a question you might find strange but it is imperative that you answer."

She placed the cup gently down on the side and turned to stare at him. "Okay?"

"I need you to please undo the left-hand cuff of your blouse and show me your arm."

She swallowed hard. She may not have been able to make many expressions with her overly Botoxed face, but her skin had turned deathly pale.

"Why on earth would you want me to undress?" she asked. Her voice was much higher than it had been a few seconds before.

"Oh no, don't undress." Swanson laughed gently, still keeping up the pretence. "Just show me your forearm please."

"Or what?" Her voice trembled.

He was right. He knew it in his veins. She knew more than she was letting on. He dropped his smile and let the anger take over. If he wasn't right, then he would have a lot of grovelling to do. He could say goodbye to his job. That was possibly gone already.

"You don't want to go there." He took a step closer to her.

"You're not from the police, are you? If so, I demand you get out of this house right now!" She pointed towards the front door, but Swanson shook his head slowly.

"I am a genuine officer, but I won't be going anywhere until you show me your forearm."

"And what if I refuse?"

"Then I'll take you to the station and you can show the nice officers there."

In the blink of an eye she was running at him waving a large carving knife above her shoulder. She was much quicker than he'd expected, but as soon as he spotted her forearm he'd been ready for her to pounce. He simply bent down to the floor, and she tripped over him, flying along the smooth kitchen tiles screaming and crying.

He ran over and pinned her to the floor, dragging the knife out from her grasp and holding both hands above her head with one of his own. She continued to scream and pulled her legs and arms away from him as he used the knife to rip open the cuff of the blouse. Then he threw it away down the other end of the room. Pulling down the sleeve, he revealed the same mark he'd found at Aunt Barb's house.

"Look at what we have here." He smiled down at her. "Found you."

She stopped screaming and her body went limp, defeated. He dragged her up from the floor and bent her over the kitchen counter to place cuffs around her wrists. She sobbed quietly to herself.

"I killed no one. I didn't," she whispered through her tears. "They made me help, but I didn't do it."

"No? Then what's the tattoo about? Did you send me the texts? Did you beat those kids who trusted you?" His voice got louder with each word.

"No! They made me," she said. "They made me. They pinned me down and forced the tattoo on me. I was stuck with them. I had to do what they said or I'd die or go to prison."

"They paid you though, didn't they?"

"Yes!" she sobbed.

"And what exactly did you do to get your paychecks from them?"

"I took evil kids to Dorothy Tilly so she could sort them out. That's it. I swear. You understand, don't you? You must see the evil ones all the time getting in trouble with the police. That's all they wanted. To get the *bad* ones out of society and get them well-trained."

"You took potential murderers to be beaten down as kids

and trained to kill," he replied. Finally, some of it made sense. "How many kids did you deliver to Tilly over the years?"

Her face hardened. "No comment."

He grinned. "That will not get you far. Do you want to know a secret? I'm not an actual officer. That was a false name. I'm going to call the police in a minute, though. I'll leave you here as a nice package for them to collect. Until they arrive, I have no rules to follow. So you better tell me how many kids you delivered."

"I don't know," she spat.

"One a month? One a year?"

"One a year." She shrugged. "I really don't remember."

"Fine. I'll leave you to the police, then."

He grabbed another set of handcuffs and dragged her to the stairwell. He stuck one cuff around her wrist and the other around a thick spindle. Once she was secure, he called Hart and disguised his phone number.

"This is an anonymous call," he said as soon as she answered.

"Swanson? What the hell are you playing at? I know it's you."

"This is an anonymous call," he repeated.

"What the hell is going on?" she snapped.

"Just listen! She has the mark on her wrist."

"Who has what mark? You aren't making any sense. Do you need me to—"

"The same mark as Marcie Livingstone."

"What? Who? What the hell is going on?"

"They're a bigger group than you police thought. Who knows how many of them there are. But I have left her handcuffed to a staircase for you to arrest."

"What the hell, Swanson! What do you mean you left her

handcuffed somewhere?" she yelled louder than he'd ever heard her yell before.

"How many times? This is an anonymous call. One person is dead. Anyone could be next. Summer. Joshua. You. I'll handcuff the entire fucking city if I need to. Now you need to come and arrest her."

"Fine. I'll leave now, Mr *Anonymous*."

She hung up, and he double checked he'd cuffed Nadene tight to the spindle before he also left. Andersson was weak. She would talk as soon as she was in an interview room. People like her always did to save their own skin. Hart would get her to talk, and he'd be ready to grab whoever else she said was involved.

25

Summer

Summer closed the laptop and stared absentmindedly around the office. It was quiet today. Only a few officers milled around. A lot were out interviewing people or doing different jobs related to the case for Aunt Barb and Mandy Harris, trying to find a connection between the two murders other than Swanson's messages.

If the press got wind of it possibly being the same killer, they'd have a field day. Summer could only imagine the terror that headlines about a suspected serial killer in Derby would cause.

Hart had rushed off somewhere after promising her an update on Dotty Foster, and that was three hours ago. It was now nearly time to pick up Joshua from her mum's house. She'd called Hart earlier but got no answer. She checked her phone again. There was nothing from her. Or from Swanson. She winced at the pain in her lip and realised she'd been biting it again.

"Summer!" a sharp voice called, making her stand up straight.

"Yes?" she said as she turned, to be presented with a pale-faced Murray.

"Where is Swanson?"

"I don't know." The look on Murray's face made Summer's heart sink. "Why? What happened?"

"Someone attacked Hart." Murray's voice broke despite the anger in her eyes. She cleared her throat. "They attacked her right on station grounds, just outside the car park."

Summer's mouth dropped open. "What? Is she badly hurt?"

"She's pretty beaten up. It is mainly nasty bruises, but she has a nasty cut on her head and appears to have a concussion. There's a possible break in her arm and in her ribs. She's knocked out with some powerful painkillers. I've not long since gotten back from the hospital. She got an anonymous call to arrest Nadene Andersson, and for some fucked up reason she went alone. Someone cuffed Andersson to her own damn stairs. She's been crying and threatening to sue the whole police force. Hart saw a tattoo on her wrist that matched Marcie Livingstone's."

Murray spat Marcie's name, having not forgiven her for being the reason Charlie Marsh was dead. Murray had little sympathy for anyone no matter how tragic their backstory was. Though station rumour had it she didn't have the nicest of childhoods herself.

"So did Andersson hurt her? Or whoever cuffed Andersson?" Summer asked. None of it made any sense. Why would Andersson have that tattoo when she was the social worker?

"No. Hart brought her back to custody and booked her in. It happened when she went out to the back car park for a smoke."

"I thought she'd quit."

"Apparently not. I looked at the CCTV and it looked like

something caught her attention at the back of the car park, and she went to investigate. She disappeared from the camera view and Rob Smith found her there twenty minutes later bleeding from her head and unconscious."

Summer cursed under her breath. Hart always seemed so invincible, but she was sweet in a Jack Russell kind of way. She'd do anything for anyone, really. Summer couldn't imagine anyone actually wanting to hurt her. "The cameras picked nothing up?"

Murray shook her head. The vein on her forehead bulged. Swanson had warned her about that vein.

"The attack happened right where the camera coverage ends."

"Like the person who did it knew," Summer muttered.

"Yes. And on that note, when did you last see Swanson?" Murray's voice hardened again.

"Swanson? This morning at his cottage," Summer replied. "Why? Does Hart need someone with her?"

Murray snorted. "Not him, that's for sure."

"What do you mean by that?" Summer responded coldly. A voice in the back of her head tried to remind her not to be rude to her new boss, but apparently her brain wasn't listening.

"He's been erratic for days, Summer. Rob Smith also saw him driving like a bloody lunatic earlier away from Derby. Who knows what frame of mind he's in?"

"He would never hurt Hart. And when I saw him this morning he was fine. Well, I made him shower and eat and *then* he was fine. But who wouldn't be a bit of a mess after finding out your closest relative has been murdered just to get to you?"

"Hmm. He needs to stay away from me and take some time off. I will find out who hurt Hart, and god help that person when I do."

Murray turned away and stormed off to her office. The door slammed behind her, making the cheap wall shake. Summer's hands trembled with quiet rage. How dare Murray silently accuse Swanson like that? He would never attack Hart no matter how stressed or upset he was.

But where was he driving like a lunatic to? What if he had lost it?

She grabbed her bag and car keys and stormed out of the station. It didn't occur to her until the door banged closed behind her that she'd parked her car in the same car park where someone had attacked Hart.

The sunlight was disappearing fast now that it was ticking past 4 p.m. But as she peered over to the back of the car park, she could see that someone had closed off a large area. Two officers were standing there with grave faces looking down at the ground and chatting in quiet voices.

Worry pulled at her. No one had seen Swanson in hours. What if they had attacked him too? Even if he was safe somewhere, he'd been driving around erratically and needed help before he got into any more trouble. She sighed heavily and made her way to the car, feeling safer with the officers standing around. There was an hour left before Joshua needed to be picked up, so there was time for a visit to Swanson's cottage. She could not let him throw his career away over this mess. Hopefully she wasn't already too late.

26

Swanson

Swanson paced the living room. His frustration with Hart's silence grew with every step. She'd promised to call him as soon as she'd spoken to Nadene Andersson, but he'd heard nothing from her so far. Maybe it meant Andersson was doing a lot of talking. He could only hope. And pace.

He jumped as someone knocked loudly on the door. Cursing himself for being so highly strung, he ran over to yank it open. He'd hoped it was Hart, but Summer stood before him, shivering in the cold.

"I wasn't expecting to see you again today," he said as she pushed past him and into the living room. He closed the door behind her wearily.

"Tough," she responded. "You're not answering your phone and someone is out there attacking people."

"That's why I've been here trying to help from afar," he replied, knowing she'd lay into him if she knew the truth. Quite rightly, probably. He flunked down onto the sofa.

"You haven't been here all day. Don't bother lying to me.

Murray said someone saw you driving like a lunatic out of the city. Where did you go?"

"That's none of your business," he snapped, the ball of fury in his chest growing more intense. He tried to remind himself that this was *Summer* he was talking to, and yet it made no difference.

"*You* are my business, Swanson. That's how relationships work. Unless you dump me right now. And even if you do, it wouldn't stop me. I will keep trying to protect you because I love you, and I don't like what Murray was insinuating about what happened to Hart."

He shot up from the chair, towering over Summer. "What happened to Hart?" His voice was low, almost like a growl.

"Hart?" Summer's face dropped as if she'd said something wrong.

"Tell me, Summer."

She took a step back from him, and guilt flooded him at scaring her. He needed to get a grip of his emotions. He closed his eyes and leaned on the bannister to put some distance between them.

"I didn't know whether to say anything. You're not exactly acting like your normal self and Murray's out for blood for whoever did it."

"I know I'm not myself right now, Summer. But I need to know what happened to Hart. Please?"

"Sit down. You need to stay calm." Summer sighed and took a seat on the opposite sofa. Only once he'd sat back down did she resume talking. "Someone attacked her in the police station car park."

He jumped straight up again with a colourful variety of curses. "Who attacked her? How badly hurt is she?"

"Sit down!" Summer pointed firmly at the sofa. He sat with his head in his hands to calm his anger before looking at her.

"Just tell me if she's okay."

"Yes. She has a concussion but is in the hospital recovering. She's going to be okay. They want to keep her for a bit. Murray said she has cuts and bruises and a sore head. Possibly a broken arm or rib they need to check out."

He breathed a heavy breath of relief and sagged back into the sofa. "So what happened to her? Was it Andersson?"

"No. Someone attacked her in the car park at the station. Hart had already booked Nadene Andersson in by then. Someone cuffed Nadene to the stairs. Hart got an anonymous call to pick her up and found she had the same tattoo as Marcie Livingstone."

"There must be CCTV of the attacker then. Who was it?"

But Summer shook her head. His fists clenched.

"How was there no CCTV?"

"It was at the back of the car park where the camera coverage ended. A blind spot."

"So it was someone who knew where the footage ends?" His brain went into overdrive. "Who would know where it ended other than someone within the station?"

Summer shrugged. "I don't know. I looked at the camera earlier. It is skewed a certain way so it doesn't face that area. It might be obvious to someone who understands CCTV and knows what to look for. You didn't seem too surprised about Andersson. How did you know Hart had gone to see her?"

"What did you mean about Murray? Did she accuse *me* of hurting Hart?"

"Not exactly." Summer hesitated. "She just said Rob Smith saw you driving like a lunatic out of Derby and she wanted to know where you went."

"What did you tell her?" he demanded.

"That you were as okay as could be expected this morning. Where did you go?"

"No, I mean what did you tell her when she insinuated I might be responsible?"

"I told her straight you wouldn't do that. I was a bit blunt to be honest. Not sure she likes me as much now."

Swanson grinned. "Good. Don't worry about it. She doesn't like anyone. I'll tell you where I went in that case, but don't freak out."

"Now I'm freaking out. Where the hell did you go?"

"I did go to see Nadene Andersson—"

"Swanson!" Summer's forehead wrinkled in annoyance.

"I know, I know. But listen, it was me that saw she has the same tattoo markings that Livingstone and Marsh had."

"Did you cuff her to the damn staircase?"

"She said someone pinned her down and forced the tattoo on her and that they said she'd lose everything if she went to the police. She didn't kill anyone, or so she said, bearing in mind she ran at me with a carving knife."

"She did what!?"

He nodded. "A giant one as if she was no stranger to violence. But what she said was that they forced her to bring the broken kids to Dorothy Tilly so she could sort them out. The point, according to her, was to make them positive members of society again. Obviously, we know that wasn't the case."

"They wanted the bad kids to hurt them. They made them obedient and scared. Taught them violence."

"Yep. As if they wanted to turn them into killers."

"So that's why you cuffed her to a spindle?"

"Only because she ran at me with the knife. I gave her a fake name."

"Wow, babe. This is serious. You could lose your job, or worse."

"I know." He shrugged. His phone buzzed on the sofa next to him. He glanced at it and shoved it into his pocket. "But I need to find out who this person is, Summer. Or I could lose more than my job."

She sighed loudly. "Maybe Billy Bailey could tell me more. I've been meaning to go and speak to him all week but things got so messy."

"It's worth a shot."

"I'll see him tomorrow. They won't let me in this late and I have to get Joshua."

He felt a sudden urge to go with her and feel Joshua's little hands wrap around his neck in a bear hug. "Tell Joshua I miss him."

She looked at him in surprise. "I will. You could always come with me to see him, you know? You are still welcome at mine and he does ask about you. I told him you've been poorly."

He shook his head gently despite the guilt that tugged at him. "I need to see Hart and then get some rest. The way I acted today was . . . erratic at best. Let me get a handle on everything first. Maybe this weekend."

"Fine." Summer stood and grabbed her handbag from the floor. "Are you sure you're going to be okay on your own? No more assaults on possible suspects?"

"Yes. I feel fine. Go on." He followed her to the front door and pulled it open. As she stepped outside, he grabbed her arm and spun her back around. He planted a kiss on her forehead and wrapped one arm around her. "Love you."

"Love you too." She squeezed him back with both arms before pulling away. "You do my head in, though. No more cuffing people, and answer your damn phone sometimes."

He grinned as she walked away. He stood at the threshold until she was in her car and waved to her as she drove off.

Because the last thing he needed was her to see where he was really going.

He'd received two texts. The first was from Simone, and she confirmed Andersson did not inherit the property at all. She purchased it herself thirty-five years previously. She used a huge deposit.

But Nadene Andersson didn't hurt Hart. She was safely locked away in the station. And yet he'd received a second text from anonymous.

You arrested the wrong person, so pretty Rebecca Hart suffered. Get it right next time.

There was only one person who he hadn't visited personally yet, and that was Ben Jackson. He was the only other person alive who knew about Charlie Marsh being dropped off at Tilly's. And seeing as someone had known exactly where the security camera footage cut off, he was long overdue for a visit.

27

Swanson

Swanson brought up the image of Ben Jackson's address from his phone, thanking his lucky stars that he'd taken the snap to show Trent the address when he'd asked her to visit him earlier in the week. Jackson had worked for Leicester police and lived about 45 minutes away just outside of Leicester city centre.

He ignored the voice nagging at him to stay inside the cottage. Or to go and see Hart or steal a cuddle from Joshua. To do anything other than visit a retired police officer acting the same way he had with Andersson. He wouldn't get away with that with Jackson.

There'd be no handcuffing him to a damn spindle, and it's not like he would've known what was going on when he took Charlie Marsh to live with Dorothy Tilly. But the man must remember something about Andersson or Tilly from that day, and anything could help at this point.

It was almost 6 p.m. by the time he was close to Leicester, and the sky was pitch black. Streetlamps guided the way as he drove off the busy dual carriageway full of rush hour traffic and down into a more secluded residential area. He checked the address. Ben lived at number 36, which ended up being a standard, semi-detached redbrick property about halfway down the street. At least it wasn't a secluded period home this time. Though there'd be more possible witnesses and CCTV, which was another reason Swanson needed to behave himself.

He pulled up right outside the house and surveyed the street as he climbed out of the car. It was an eerily quiet road. Even though most people would be back from work by this time, eating dinner with their families, probably. His stomach suddenly growled at him. He tried to think if he'd eaten anything since Summer's bacon sandwiches, but yet again the day had passed in an angry blur.

He ignored the growl and stepped onto the pavement. Ben's house had four foot fencing around the front garden and a small gate in the middle. Swanson opened the gate and glanced at the garden. There was a stretch of immaculately trimmed grass on either side of the slabbed pathway, which led to a brown front door. What's with these people and their perfect gardens? He'd never seen so many.

It wasn't until he knocked loudly on the door that he realised he had no plan. His thoughts on the drive here were consumed with anger at whoever had hurt Hart and murdered Barb. But when the door opened, he still had nothing. So he acted on impulse and forced a wide smile at the tall man in front of him. It wasn't often someone made Swanson feel small, but this guy was huge despite getting on in age.

"Mr Jackson?" he asked.

"Yes?" The man looked at him suspiciously. Much as he'd expect an ex-officer to do.

"I'm Detective Inspector Alex Swanson." He flashed his ID.

There was no point lying about who he was to an experienced police officer. Let Murray hear about it and sack him. What did it matter? "Can I come in?"

To his relief, Jackson smiled as soon as he saw the police ID. "Of course. Come in."

He took a step back to allow Swanson to walk inside. The hallway was modern and bright with a staircase directly in front of the door.

"Please, take a seat." Ben pointed to a door on his left and Swanson walked into a living room with light grey walls and a smart wooden floor. He took a seat at the end of the grey sofa and moved a matching cushion out of his way as he sat back.

Jackson relaxed into an armchair across from Swanson. It was the opposite of the tense or angry reactions Swanson usually received. But not surprising from a fellow officer, retired or not.

"Would you like a drink?" Jackson asked.

Swanson shook his head. "No thanks. I don't have much time actually. I believe one of our officers visited you the other day?"

"Yes. Lisa Trent. She wanted to chat about an old foster kid case."

"Yes. She said you couldn't remember it. Is that correct?"

Ben nodded. "I did say that at the time, but I have remembered bits of it since she visited. I was going to call her to chat about it. It was an awful case. I think I'd blocked it from memory."

"What did you remember?"

Ben uncrossed his legs and leaned forward, elbows on his knees. "The same night your officer visited me I had a dream. Well, it was more of a nightmare, really."

"Was it normal back then for police to attend such a visit?" Swanson asked.

"It could be. It depended on the situation and on availability. The system was more . . . harsh back then. I hope it's nicer these days." He shuddered and leaned back again.

"Sorry for interrupting. You were telling me about the dream?"

"Yes. It brought everything back from meeting that little girl."

"What did you think of her?"

"The girl? She was a skinny little thing. They blamed her for the death of her parents, but there was no proof. The social worker seemed scared of her. I didn't feel any evilness from her. She was quiet. Reserved. I think presenting that way puts people off guard sometimes. I could see she was hurting. It haunted me, dropping her off in a place she'd never even visited, but her foster mother seemed lovely. I remember she was an older lady. Probably dead by now. She'd baked homemade pie to welcome the little girl."

"Her foster mother was abusive."

His head tilted and a look of surprise crossed his face. "That woman was abusive?"

"She beat them and her boyfriend sexually abused them," Swanson replied. He was baiting for a reaction, and he watched Jackson's body language closely. His skin paled. His hand flew to his stomach.

"No," he whispered. "Those poor children."

"The girls murdered her in the end," Swanson continued. "And her boyfriend."

Ben's eyes widened. "Christ. That's awful. Those poor kids. What a mess. I've heard and seen some awful things as an officer, but that's made me feel hot and bothered, truth be told."

Jackson pulled up the sleeves of his top to his elbow. Swanson immediately searched his skin, but there was no mark on his inner forearm or anywhere else. He didn't have Nadene Andersson's attitude towards the kids. He was as sickened by it as anyone would be. He was just a normal officer. This was a waste of time. There must be someone else he was missing.

"Is there anything else you can remember about the case?" he asked hopefully.

"That's it I'm afraid. I wasn't involved past that. Unless there's something in particular you wanted to ask me about? It might jog my memory."

"That was it from me. Thanks for your time, Mr Jackson." Swanson stood to leave. Jackson followed.

"No problem. If I remember anything else I will call the station to speak to you."

"Perfect. Just ask for Lisa Trent instead. I'll probably be out."

Jackson reached out to shake his hand. Swanson obliged, but the man kept a strong grip of his hand.

"This job can get you down sometimes. Make sure you look after yourself and your family."

"I do." Swanson moved to take his hand away, but he tightened his grip.

"I'm serious, young man. There's nothing more important than family, especially not work. And I can spot a stressed officer when I see one."

A lump grew in Swanson's throat at the thought of Aunt Barb. Jackson was right. The job wasn't worth what happened to her, but it was too late for that. He pulled his hand from Ben's grasp and swallowed hard as they walked to the front door.

"Nice to meet you," he said out of habit when he stepped through the front door.

"Nice to meet you. Remember what I said."

Jackson closed the door behind him and Swanson returned slowly back to the car. He'd thought visiting Jackson had been a waste of time, but the muddled feeling in his head had disappeared. His thoughts were much clearer than when he arrived.

What Ben Jackson had said was simple. He needed to quit before more people got hurt. What if it was Summer lying dead in a ditch? Leaving Joshua without a mother. Or Joshua himself could get hurt. Nothing was worth losing either of them.

He got in the car and headed back home to the cottage. But when he entered Derby half an hour later, he changed direction and ended up at the police station.

He barely remembered getting in the car, never mind driving there. But he knew what he had to do. It was just past 8 p.m., but Murray would be in. She lived there when a big case was going on. He was numb as he walked to her office.

There was no point knocking. The fear of being fired had disappeared. He simply walked straight in.

"Swanson! What the hell?" Murray was behind her desk, pulling on her coat. "I was about to give up on finding you."

"I quit," he replied.

"Don't be stupid," she replied without missing a beat.

"What?" He looked over at her, bewildered.

"I won't be accepting your notice, thank you. You look like shit. Go home and have a rest."

"Earlier I went to Nadene Andersson's house. I handcuffed her to the stair spindle and told Hart anonymously to pick her up. I just visited Ben Jackson thinking he might be involved.

He's a police officer for god's sake. I've lost it, Murray. My aunt's dead. Hart's in hospital. Summer or Joshua could be next. I'm done."

"What the fuck, Swanson?" Murray said through gritted teeth. "I heard none of that. I heard nothing. You need to mourn. Go home and take a break. Stop doing stupid things. I don't want to see you around here for at least a week."

"I'm quitting."

"No. You'll make that decision *after* a rest. Now tell Trent what Ben Jackson said and she can carry on your work while Hart isn't here."

"But—"

"No buts. Get the hell out and don't speak to me for a week."

She shooed him away from her desk and out the door. He stood outside, still bewildered by her reaction. So much for thinking she'd be ecstatic if he quit.

He forced his legs to move to Trent's office. He couldn't tell her about Andersson. Trent would grass him up the second she knew what he'd done. She followed the rules to a T. Other than that she was the only other officer he knew of who had also swindled a bit of an office in the older part of the building.

He knocked gently on her makeshift office door, but there was no response. She was probably home by now and trying to rest with her family. It was probably best to leave a sticky note rather than text her. At least that wouldn't disturb her.

He let himself in and grabbed the small stack of yellow sticky notes that sat in front of the monitor. He searched around the desk for a pen to no avail. He yanked open the top drawer to find one, but his fingers folded around a photo instead.

Curiosity got the better of him, and he pulled it out of the drawer.

It was a picture of a younger Lisa Trent. An older man had his arm around her. They were smiling from some sort of balcony; the sea sat behind him.

Swanson squinted at the photo. He recognised that face.

A man she never admitted that she knew, and yet went to interview him.

The same man Swanson had just spoken to.

Ben Jackson.

28

Summer

Summer settled onto the sofa and pulled the soft blanket around her. She flicked on the TV, paying no attention to what appeared on screen but enjoying the background noise all the same, and scrolled through her phone.

Swanson weighed heavily on her mind. He was such a closed book. He never accepted help from anyone, never talked about his feelings. Or rarely, at least. He didn't seem interested in opening up to her at all. She couldn't decide if it was her fault for being too clingy in trying to make sure he was okay. Or if that's just how he was. Maybe she wasn't clingy enough. Her finger hovered over his name in her phone.

"Mummy!" Joshua yelled from his bedroom.

Great. The neighbours will love listening to that.

"Come here if you need me," she called back for at least the fifth time that week. The walls were thin, and the neighbours were grumpy. The last thing she needed was a noise complaint if she was going to ask to renew the lease. And that was looking more likely with Swanson being in a spiral of grief. Who could blame him?

The pitter patter of small feet made her smile as she waited for his face to appear in the doorway. She might crave peace but he was so damn cute in his new football pyjamas with his brown hair sticking out all over the place. He stood in the hallway holding on tight to Everest, his little husky teddy. His bottom lip stuck out and he stared at her with serious blue eyes.

"What's wrong, babe?" She held her arms out for a hug and he wandered over and climbed onto her knee.

"I can't find my Harry Potter wand," he said in a small voice.

"Oh no. It's on your desk." She wrapped her arms tightly around him. "But it's time for sleep, anyway."

"It's not! I've checked there already. I won't be able to sleep until I know where it is!"

"You haven't played with it in months!"

"But I really do need it." He pulled away from her grip and crossed his arms in protest. His bottom lip quivered. She sighed.

"Come on. I'll find it, and then you need to sleep. No playing with it until tomorrow."

"Thank you, Mummy!" He threw his arms around her neck and squeezed tight. "I love you!"

"All right! Don't choke me."

She picked him up and carried him to his room. She groaned under the weight, he was getting far too big, and placed him heavily on his bed. The wand was on his desk, underneath a T-shirt he'd thrown on top of it at some point. It clearly hadn't crossed his mind to move anything.

"Can you sleep now?" she asked as she tucked him into the bedsheets.

"Yes, Mummy! You're the best. Love you."

"Love you too. Good night."

She kissed his forehead and tried to go back to doom scrolling in front of the TV, but a text had actually popped up from Murray.

Keep an eye on Swanson. Don't let him anywhere near work. He needs a break before he does something stupid.

She closed her eyes. What the hell had he done now? She was well aware he needed a break. In fact, the only person who did not seem to realise that was Swanson himself. Those stupid messages he kept getting were not helping. She briefly considered asking him to hand the phone in to Murray. He could get a new one and pretend they weren't happening. Murray and the team could investigate the murders. Swanson could rest his brain.

But he'd never go for that.

Screw it.

She pressed the Call icon before she could second guess herself again. He'd either answer or he wouldn't. No big deal. At least he'd know she cared enough to call. When he answered straight away, she was unprepared.

"Summer? Are you there?" he repeated.

"Yes, sorry. I'm here. Just calling to chat. You okay?" she replied.

"Yes. I'm fine. You don't need to keep asking. I promise I'm all right." He actually sounded weirdly chirpy.

"You sound . . . happy," she said cautiously.

He laughed darkly. "I wouldn't say that. But I have just found something that might help us out."

"Oh, Swanson! You're supposed to be at home resting."

"And I was on my way home! Murray asked me to leave Lisa Trent a note with what to look into before I went home."

"What were you even doing with Murray if you've been at

home?" she asked.

He hesitated. "Nothing important."

"Hmm."

"So I went to Trent's office, and, Summer, I think she's our guy."

Summer sat forward on the sofa, head in her hands. "What could possibly make you believe that, babe? This is Lisa Trent we're talking about."

There was a brief silence before he responded. "You don't believe me. Everyone thinks I've gone mad with grief."

"That's not what I said, but listen to what you just told me. Lisa Trent? Miss serious *follows the law to the letter* Trent is a bad guy!"

"She knows Ben Jackson, Summer! How? Why didn't she tell us? She's the one who went to interview him."

"How are they related?"

"I don't know! Ask her. I saw a photo in her desk drawer."

"In her drawer? Is it the same one that was on her desk before? That's a photo of her and her dad!" Summer thought back to the time she'd smiled at the photo and Trent had proudly told her about her father. "He's an ex-police officer."

"He's Ben Jackson."

"Have you ever even met Ben Jackson? How do you know it's him?"

Swanson cursed loudly. "I just know, Summer. Isn't that enough?"

"And I just know that you've been through a lot. Isn't that enough to come and sit with me for a bit and talk through this properly?"

"If you don't believe me then what's the point?" he snapped.

The line went dead. He'd actually hung up on her. Summer

threw the phone on the sofa in frustration. Every bone in her body ached to check on him, but Joshua was too young to be left alone.

She needed to chat with someone who knew him. Someone like Hart, except she was still in hospital. The only other person she had a phone number for was Murray. He'd hate her for it, but someone needed to stop him before he ended his career, and who better than his boss?

29

Swanson

Swanson cancelled Murray's call again and swallowed down the disgusting hot liquid in his cup. Whatever she wanted to yell at him about could wait. He'd never been a fan of any hot drinks, but coffee was the worst of the lot. The taste, the smell, and the heartburn. Not to mention the stomach cramps. But so many people he knew swore by coffee to keep them awake, and he had no time for sleep. A plan needed to be made.

He laid out his notebook on the table and scribbled furiously, starting with names, places, and connections. Motive made him pause. What possible motive could any of these people have for murdering poor Barb? Or even for hurting him? Out of the list of suspects, the only person who knew him was Lisa Trent, and they'd always gotten along fine. Yet she hid being related to Ben Jackson. He'd always thought she knocked on his office door to be polite, but he realised now she did that to see if he was inside. Then there was his chair always being the wrong height. She'd been sitting at his desk and looking through his things. It was all clicking together piece by piece.

She was easy to get along with. Trent had a reputation for being hard-faced but she was excellent at the job. She loved it. He sat back on the sofa and rubbed his fingers through his beard, which was becoming scruffy as hell. Not one instance of upsetting her came to mind. Certainly nothing big enough to warrant killing his aunt or hurting Hart.

But he remembered a time when he'd given her a lift home after an issue with her car. That was only a year ago. She probably still lived in the same place. But he'd need a new car if he was going to her house. She'd recognise his Audi too easily. He scoured the couch for his phone, finally finding it on the floor, and hit Call.

"Hello? It's me," he said.

"Yes, Alex. I know it's you," his mother replied, still slightly cold after their previous conversation.

"I need to swap our cars. Well, I need to borrow yours. You can borrow mine too, though. Don't worry."

He waited a moment, but she met his words with silence. He brought the phone away from his ear to check the screen, but she was still there.

"Can you hear me?" he asked.

"Yes, I'm here. I just don't know what to say. Why on earth would you want my car? It doesn't exactly suit you."

"I just need it for tonight. I'll come round in five minutes."

He hung up the call and made a whole flask of disgusting coffee before setting off to her house. She only lived a few streets away. He vaguely wondered if she'd force herself into his life more now that Barb was dead, but he pushed the thoughts away. It was too hard to think about that and the plan at the same time. That's why it was good to keep busy. Overthinking never helped anyone.

He pulled up to his mother's house and parked his car on the street a few houses away. The new-build homes on her street were small, horrible things. He'd never have a new build; they were cheaply built and cramped, but his mum seemed to love it. It was the first time in years she'd had her own space. All the new properties on this road had a one-car driveway. Which made no sense to Swanson. How many families in this day and age had only one car? So he abandoned his halfway up the street and knocked on her door.

She answered quickly, she'd obviously been waiting for him to arrive. Her car keys were in her hand and she passed them to him without a word. He tried to give her his key in return.

"Ooh, no." She gently pushed his hand away. "I don't think I could drive your car. It's far too big."

"Just take the key anyway. Just in case. It's not like you need to race anywhere in it."

"What if I scratch a tire or something?"

The smell of beef stew wafted out from behind his mother, and he took a moment to inhale it. It was one smell that always reminded him of her and one of the few happy times they had together. She always made stew when she was happy when he was a kid. Though she surely wasn't happy after finding out about Barb.

"Why are you making stew?" he asked.

She sighed heavily, and then swallowed. Tears pinched her eyes. "It reminds me of being a kid with her."

The smell made him want to go inside and do something simple like laugh together as they watched TV. But only for a nanosecond. He had to make this right first.

"I'm going to get them, Mum. And I don't care about the car. Here." He shoved the key into her hand. "I have to go."

"Wait! Where are you going? You haven't told me why you need my car."

"It's just work. My car won't do because the suspect knows what it looks like," he explained.

"Suspect?" she asked, the worry clear in her tone.

"You'll be helping me find out who hurt Barb." He smiled at her, and she gave him a determined nod.

"Okay, Alex. As long as you're careful."

"I won't hurt the car, don't worry," he replied as he turned to get into her black Toyota Yaris. No way would anyone suspect him of driving such a small car.

"I meant to be careful of yourself! I don't care about the car, either. As long as you're okay. I can't lose you, too."

He glanced back at her. She looked frail in her dressing gown and soft slippers, and she shivered at the frigid December air. And he realised that no matter what had gone on between them in the past, he needed to protect her, too.

"I'll be fine. Close the door, it's freezing."

She nodded sadly and closed the door. He climbed into the Yaris and suddenly felt very snug with his head only an inch away from hitting the ceiling. He turned the engine on straight away, blasting up the heaters to warm through his freezing backside.

The seat was so close to the pedals a damn hobbit could drive the car. He fiddled with the buttons on the side of the driver's seat to push it back into a normal man position that wouldn't severely cramp his legs, then threw his backpack onto the front passenger seat.

That would usually be Hart's seat on such a stakeout. She'd understand the connection to Trent if she wasn't in hospital. Although she'd probably side with bloody Murray.

He suddenly remembered Murray's missed calls from earlier and quickly glanced at his phone as he clicked the seat belt into place. There were no additional missed calls but there was a text message from her.

You're suspended. Don't come in to work.

He threw the phone back down. What was up with her? She didn't want him to quit but then suspended him? She couldn't suspend him without some sort of investigation or trial, surely. And anyway, it didn't matter at that point.

He pulled off the tiny drive and made his way back into the city. Trent lived in a terraced house that was not too far from the station itself. It was close to Markeaton Park, which he passed as he pulled off the Markeaton Island roundabout at Ashbourne Road. A sadness hit him as he passed the park. He was always trying to convince Barb to meet him there, and she always refused because she preferred the Darley Abbey park.

The hurt pushed him on, and he pulled off the main road and onto the side street where Trent's small house was located. He pulled up on the side of the road a few houses down from hers. The houses on the street did not have driveways, and instead the front doors led straight on to the pavement. So the Yaris fit in nicely on the street. No way would Trent suspect it was him.

All of Trent's curtains were closed, though there was a light on in the front room. In most of these types of houses that would be the living room. He pulled his notepad, pen, and flask of coffee out of the backpack on the front seat. They were in for a long night, but if he wasn't allowed into work anyway, then at least he could give Trent all of his attention. Hart was in hospital and Summer wanted nothing to do with it. It was just him and Trent and the coffee. He sat back and got comfy, readying himself for a long night.

30

Swanson

S wanson woke up with a start. His head banged off the car window, and his knees collided with the steering wheel. He groaned in pain as he rubbed his head and forced himself to sit up straight.

Weak sunlight blurred his vision, and it took his brain a moment to catch up and realise that he was still in his mothers Yaris. Clearly the coffee hadn't been as effective as he'd hoped. His fingers were icy, despite the thick gloves he'd found in the front compartment, and he couldn't feel his toes. He flicked on the engine and turned up the heat. The clock on the car's dashboard read just past 8 a.m.

He rubbed his eyes hard to clear his vision and looked over at Trent's house. The curtains remained closed, and there was no movement that he could see. But her car was still parked up on the road outside. He searched through empty packets of crisps and biscuits on the front seat, throwing them to the ground in an effort to find his phone to confirm the time. God knows if his mum had ever made sure the clock in the car was correct.

He finally found both phones under the backpack and confirmed the car clock was correct. Trent usually got into work around 8:30. So she should leave her house within the next fifteen minutes. The noise of a door being shut brought his attention back to the street. A rush of adrenaline hit him as he saw Trent locking up her front door. Like usual, she was as neat as a pin, despite not yet wearing her police uniform. She wore black trousers under a dark puffy coat.

He stared at her as she struggled with turning the key in the old lock. Now that she was in front of him, it struck him what he was actually doing. Trent was always so serious about her job. She loved helping people. Was he really about to follow her?

The beep of her car unlocking brought him to his senses. Hart couldn't investigate her from the hospital bed, and Murray and Summer wouldn't listen to him—it was obvious they thought he was losing the plot. He had no choice but to follow Trent.

He pulled the seat belt over his shoulder and drew his woolly hat down his head. Though she'd be unlikely to recognise him from such a distance, especially in such a tiny car. Better to be safe than sorry. Trent's car pulled off the street, and he followed quite a way behind until they reached the main road.

The traffic at this time in the city was the worst during the working week. Usually it would wind him up to no end. But it made it easy to find cars to hide behind as he followed Trent, and it meant she couldn't drive too quickly. She weaved through the packed roundabouts and down the dual carriageway. Which was strange because the road headed away from the station.

Where the hell is she going?

She actually drove all the way through the city to Chaddesden, or *Chad* to locals, close to Pride Park Stadium where footballers either delighted or embarrassed the city each week. It was nowhere near the police station.

When she reached a side street, the bulk of the traffic dispersed and he had to be more careful not to be seen. He pulled up at the end and watched her turn left before he turned down the same road himself. She pulled up outside someone's house, and it crossed his mind briefly that it might be related to the case. But there was no one involved that he could think of who had a Chad address.

She was now quite far down the street, and he squinted to see what she did. She walked up to one house, and to his surprise she didn't knock before she let herself straight into the property. Did she have a second home right near the first one? Why would she bother?

Maybe she rented it out, but then she wouldn't be able to just walk right in like that as a landlord. Trent disappeared inside. A figure stood outside the door and looked up and down the street. Swanson stared, squinting harder, but he would have sworn on his life that the figure was Ben Jackson.

Or he really was losing the plot.

The figure also disappeared inside, and Swanson clicked off his seat belt. He got out of the car and hurried down the street, trying not to look suspicious. At least the wintry morning meant he could pull his hood right over his face without looking dodgy. In this weather his tracksuit bottoms and woolly hat made him look like most other men walking around casually. It was much harder to look casual in his usual suit based attire.

Three houses away from the one Trent disappeared into, he stopped and pretended to be looking at something on his phone. He raised his eyes to peer at the house. He needed a way in. This might be crazy, but he had to know what they were talking about.

He took a few steps forward, still pretending to be looking down at his phone. There was movement in the upstairs window on the right-hand side. Nothing from the downstairs windows from where he stood.

Fuck it.

He walked casually up to the front door just like Trent had done. He kept his head down and hood up so no camera would pick up his face, but by the time he reached the door it was locked. Cursing, he moved back around to the side of the house. The small gate opened easily, and he snuck around to the back door. The rear garden was a mess of long grass and weeds. A rusted table and chairs sat in the middle of the grass, and a fridge long past its glory days was thrown in a corner. But he grinned when he noticed the back door was actually ajar.

He listened next to the door. No noise came from inside. He pushed it open and stepped straight into the kitchen. Wet washing was strewn all over the chairs and one radiator, and the kitchen counter was a mess with piles of dishes and a previous dinner all over the side.

Voices came from upstairs. One he recognised instantly as Lisa Trent's. He sneaked forward to hear what they were saying but froze when he heard footsteps. The voices became clearer as they reached the top of the stairs, and he dashed back into the kitchen.

He pulled out his work phone and called his personal mobile before leaving the work phone on the messy countertop. Then he ran out of the kitchen and around the side of the house, forcing himself to stop there. He searched around the external wall of the house for obvious cameras but could see nothing.

No one would see the phone he'd left in that mess. Trent

might even think she'd left it if they found it. Their standard issue work phones mostly looked the same. He held his phone to his ear and listened intently as he crouched down at the side of the property.

"This place is a mess." He recognised Trent's voice instantly. "But it will do. It's just an old suspect's house who owes me a favour."

"Never mind that. Is Swanson doing what we need him to?"

Swanson felt the adrenaline rush through him as he heard Ben Jackson's voice. He'd been right. They were both fully involved in this mess.

"He's gone AWOL, according to Murray. Killing his aunt might have been too much," replied Trent. She didn't sound angry or sad. Her voice was the usual monotone voice she presented.

"He has Nadene instead. That wasn't supposed to happen."

"That was her own fault." Jackson's calm voice was much like Trent's. Devoid of emotion. "He does not know about you and he doesn't suspect me of anything."

"Nadene can take the blame for the murders," Trent replied. "I'll push him towards her and her and that's it. The other one can take the blame for the messages. Then she will be out of our lives. Now I need to get to work. I'll call later."

The voices lowered as they all walked with Trent to the front of the house. Swanson snuck back around to peer through the door. The kitchen was empty. He stepped in to retrieve his phone and ran back to the side.

He crouched low so Trent couldn't see him, but he could see her. She waved goodbye and got back into her car. Jackson disappeared back inside and shut the front door with a bang, and Swanson waited a few tense seconds before sneaking back down the front driveway. He walked casually up the road and flicked the engine on as soon as he got back into the car.

He didn't move once in the car. He tried to comprehend what he had just heard. Trent really was involved. She knew who'd killed Barb. She'd known the whole time. And it sounded like she was the one sending him messages.

His face felt a sudden warmth, and he realised tears were wetting his cheeks. He wiped them away. This was no time to be emotional. He had to focus. Trent would pay, and so would Ben Jackson. This network was getting bigger and bigger. But they'd made a huge mistake. It was time for it to come crashing down.

31

Summer

Summer's boots thudded off the marble staircase as she ran down them. The lack of sleep from worrying about Swanson had led her to not hear the alarm at 7 a.m. Luckily, Mum had left twenty minutes ago with Joshua to take him to school so she could go straight to the station. Being so late only three months into a new job was hardly a good look.

She pulled open the heavy front doors of the building and was greeted with the freezing morning air as she ran through the threshold. She carried on running to her car but cursed as she realised she hadn't closed the stupid doors and ran back to slam them shut.

Her breath was heavy as she scurried back to the car park. But she stopped in her tracks just before she reached the car. A man was leaning on her bonnet in dark tracksuit bottoms and a black coat. He stared down at the ground with his hood pulled over his face. She took a few steps backwards, ready to run. The man suddenly looked up as if she'd startled him, and the recognition hit her.

"Swanson?" she whispered in disbelief.

His eyes were bloodshot with heavy black bags. His skin was almost as pale as hers, and she never saw him during the working week without his suit unless he was in the cottage after work.

"Hi, Summer," he replied. His voice was low and cold.

"Are you okay?" she asked. He shook his head, and she stepped slowly towards him. "What is it? Has something else happened?"

"I need your help with something," he said. He pulled out his phone and showed her the screen.

Still not there yet, Swanson. Hurry up or Summer's next.

Summer's stomach went cold at the thought of Joshua being in danger. "What do you need from me?"

"You have a choice. I can drive you somewhere safe." Swanson pushed the phone back into his pocket. "Or you can be bait. But I'll be right behind you everywhere you go."

"Bait?" Summer repeated incredulously.

"You just go about your normal day, but I'll be right behind you in this." He nodded towards the Yaris.

Summer stared at the tiny car. No words came to her. *Had he had a complete breakdown?* The freezing wind picked up and howled quietly around them. She sucked in a breath at the iciness. Swanson didn't react to it at all. He simply stared at her.

"Where's your car?" she asked eventually.

"I swapped it for my mother's."

He said it so casually that it caused her concern to increase tenfold.

"Are you sure you're thinking straight? I can't imagine you without your car."

"Yes. That is proof I'm thinking straight. I couldn't follow anyone in the Audi. Everyone knows it's mine."

"Who have you been following?" she asked gently.

He sighed and leaned against her car. "I will tell you but you can't go mad at me."

"I can't promise that until I know, can I?" she snapped. "Just spit it out."

"You are turning more and more into Hart, you know that?" he snapped back. "I knew there was something strange about Trent after she hid the fact that Ben Jackson is her dad. So last night I had the idea to watch her house, and this morning I followed her. She ended up going to a house in Chad, and guess who was there."

Summer threw her hands in the air. He tutted at her lack of participation.

"Ben Jackson!" he revealed with a dark grin.

"And what does that tell us?"

"Nothing much in itself. Except I snuck in and planted my phone so I could hear what they said—"

"You didn't!" Summer interrupted. "Why on earth would you risk your job like that?"

His eyes hardened. "My aunt is dead, Summer. You and Joshua are being threatened. This is not about my job. This is personal."

"But you will still lose the career you've worked so hard for! That might be what Trent wants if she is involved. Maybe it's jealousy."

"Barb died because of my job. Hart's in hospital. I don't care if I lose it. I care about finding these evil bastards and putting them away before they get to you."

"They'll get away with it at this rate and you know it. If this goes to court with all of this messing around you're doing, then it will be *case dismissed.*" She waved her hand to push the point, but he stared at her blankly.

"Murray has made me promise to stay away from the station. No one knows what I've done other than you, and to make sure it gets through court, we need to make sure we gather actual proof. Me following you to make sure you're okay once I've received this text would be fine. That's what a normal person would do. I'd catch them in action, arrest them, job done."

"Would they? I think they'd call the police and trust them to protect both of us."

"That isn't an option."

"How can I believe you when you're acting like this and you look like shit? Just come back with me. Shower, sleep, and eat. *Then* we'll talk."

"I don't need—"

"Stop. Accept my help, otherwise I will tell Murray right now that you need help from someone else. I am not leaving you alone in this bloody state." She turned to walk back to the flat. "Come on."

She heard him curse, but his footsteps soon followed. She texted Murray as she walked to let her know she was keeping Swanson out of trouble and wouldn't be in the station. That would keep her off their backs for the day at least. And that way she'd have time to figure out how to help Swanson. If anyone was still after either of them, they could tackle them together.

32

Swanson

Swanson sat back on Summer's soft sofa. She'd agreed to be bait only if he got his strength up enough to protect her. Which was ridiculous because he would always have the strength to protect both her and Joshua. Though he had to admit he looked like crap when he saw himself in her bathroom mirror.

She'd also forced a whole plate of bacon sandwiches down him. But as he waited for her to get ready, his eyes got heavy. He blinked hard to keep them open, only to find them closing again seconds later. He rested peacefully at first as the darkness settled around him. There was a calmness to it. His brain had finally switched off.

Then the pale hands came reaching out from the pitch black corners of Summer's living room. They grabbed at his legs, moving up to his torso. He tried to reach out to fight them off but he couldn't move. He couldn't shout. They had no bodies or faces. They were just unknown hands reaching out to pull him down. He didn't know where they wanted to take him, but he knew it was a dark place that he would never escape from.

One hand moved up to wrap around his neck.

A bang made him jump up from the sofa, and the hands disappeared. Summer's living room was normal and bright again. He panted heavily. Sweat fell from his forehead. There were no hands. And no Summer.

"Summer?" he yelled as he forced his legs to move forward to look in the kitchen.

He ran around the small flat searching every room, but Summer was nowhere to be found. His phone was on the coffee table, and he picked it up to call her. But an unread text from her flashed up.

Just popping over to visit Hart. I didn't want to wake you. You looked like you needed some rest. We can make a plan together soon. You're not alone in this. Love you.

He growled in frustration. If the evil bastards got her too, he would murder every one of them with his bare hands. Summer had only sent the text one minute ago. The bang that woke him must have been her closing the damn door. He grabbed his coat and backpack and ran to the window—her car was only just pulling off from the parking space.

He ran out of the flat and down the marble staircase, regretting the bacon now that his body was apparently too old to digest meat without severe heartburn. He panted heavily by the time he reached the Yaris. He suddenly regretted not having the much more powerful Audi that still sat on his mum's road; probably untouched.

He jumped into the car and threw his backpack onto the front seat. He turned left out of the car park, pulling the seat belt over his body as he drove to stop the incessant beeping the car would do until the seat belt clicked into place.

He turned right onto the main road and spotted Summer's

car stuck at the red lights further up. Thanks to the traffic he was about ten cars behind her, but at least she wouldn't see him. This would be fine in court. He was off duty, and just making sure his partner was okay after a threatening text. Her text to him even proved it.

He followed Summer onto the ring road that ran around the city to the hospital. Other cars pulled off in different directions and only five vehicles ended up in between them. Because she knew the city well, Summer escaped from the ring road and turned right onto Ashbourne Road and then left to cut out the main traffic. The other cars all pulled off in different directions, except for one.

The silver jeep in front of him had also followed Summer religiously. Swanson held back. He allowed another car to get in front of him and the jeep as they returned to the dual carriageway that led straight to the hospital. The jeep followed Summer all the way into the hospital entrance. She continued to drive around the outside of the hospital.

The jeep followed.

Swanson was too far back to see who was in it. But there were about eight different car parks at the hospital depending on which bit you were visiting. It would be a highly unusual coincidence if they'd been going to the same car park as Summer after being right behind her since the flat in Mickleover.

Summer continued straight past the final car park and pulled out of a rear service exit of the hospital. No one should use that exit.

But again the jeep followed.

He slammed his foot down on the accelerator and sped up to keep close, no longer caring if the jeep noticed him. He grabbed his phone and called Summer.

"Swanson? I'm at the hospital. Someone's following me," she cried. "What do I do?"

"It's okay. I'm right behind you. Don't panic, you're doing great."

"You are? I didn't even spot you. It's the jeep. Can you see it? I even pulled back out of the hospital and it's still on my tail."

"Pull over. You're right near Nixt Street. It's quiet there."

"Are you sure? Where are you?"

"I'm right behind the jeep, babe. I've got you."

Summer sighed. "Okay. Stay on the phone with me please."

"Of course. I'm just pulling out of the hospital now. Have you pulled over?"

"Yes."

"Keep the doors locked. What's the jeep doing?"

"Oh, they've driven past me."

"Can you see who's in it?"

"No. They had a hat pulled right down. Wait. They've pulled up in front of me."

"I'm just turning onto the road now. Don't panic. I can see you. I'm coming."

Every nerve in his body was on fire as he pulled the Yaris onto Nixt Road behind a van.

"I'm going to get out," Summer said.

"No. That wasn't the plan," he snapped. "Stay inside with the doors locked."

"That won't prove anything, Swanson. Other than that someone was following me and that's hard to prove. If they try to hurt me, you've got them. You can arrest them."

"It's not worth it, Summer. Stay in the—"

The line went dead. He jumped out of the Yaris cursing and stuck his head around the van to see what was happening.

Summer had already jumped out of the car. And the figure from the jeep was hurrying her with a flash of something metal in their hand.

Swanson ran. Screw being seen. The figure didn't notice him, they were too focused on their target. But they were much closer to where Summer stood.

And they reached her first.

Their hand flew backwards and the carving knife held within it became clear as day. His heart nearly burst from running so quickly towards them. But he needn't have panicked.

Summer simply bent down, and the person tripped right over her. It was the same trick he'd taught her last year. A laugh escaped him as he watched them fall, and he was filled with pride.

A colourful range of curses escaped from the attacker as they fell to the ground. The knife clattered from their hand and onto the ground where Summer kicked it away. Someone behind them screamed, and he heard Summer trying to explain they were police officers and not to panic.

He dragged the attacker up from the ground and round and threw them against Summer's car, pinning their hands behind their back.

"Get the fuck off me!"

It was a woman's voice; a familiar voice which he couldn't quite place. He pinned her hands and held her body against the car. And as he reached up to pull off the hat that hid her face, he almost let go in shock.

33

Swanson

"What the fuck?" Swanson whispered.

"Who the hell is that?" Summer cried from behind him. "I've never seen her before in my life!"

"Dotty Foster. The sister of Mandy Harris. Call the station. We need a squad car. Make it clear not to send Lisa Trent to pick her up."

Dotty Foster wailed as he held her against the bonnet of the car. "I didn't want to hurt anyone!"

"You can explain that in court," he spat.

She didn't say another word and sobbed quietly as they waited for the car to pick her up. It didn't take long to arrive, sirens blaring as it came down the street. Two men jumped out and ran over to Swanson. He explained who she was and that she'd followed Summer and then attacked her with a knife. A witness from the adjacent house also spoke to them to back up Swanson's story.

The officers cuffed Foster and placed her in the back of their car. One of them bagged up the knife before they left to take her back to the station.

Swanson looked over as Summer walked over to him. He noticed her hands still trembled and placed his arm around her.

"You were amazing," he said. "You used my trick."

"Thanks." She leaned into his chest. "I was only that brave because you were there."

He pointed at her car. "Are you going to be okay to drive back to the station? We'll need a proper witness statement."

She nodded and pulled away from him. "Let's do it quickly before I change my mind."

"Good. I'll be right behind you."

The drive to the station was a short one. It passed by in a blur. He followed closely behind Summer to make sure she knew he was right there. She looked continuously for him in her rearview mirror, and his stomach clenched as he realised he nearly lost her because of his own carelessness in asking her to be bait.

When they reached the station grounds, the squad car pulled up in the side entrance to bring Dotty Foster in. An officer opened her door, and Swanson glanced at her as he drove by. The tears still fell. She looked pretty innocent and pathetic. If it hadn't been for Summer and an independent witness, no one would've believed that she was so violent.

Summer parked first, and he rolled in behind her. At least he could park the little Yaris anywhere. It fit in any space without issue. She trudged over to him as he got out of the car. He wrapped his arms around her again and then grabbed her hand and led her up the steps to the door. A sense of peace he hadn't felt in days washed over him knowing that she was safe.

For now.

They'd caught one of them, but there was a lot of work to do yet to get some actual answers. He paused before pushing open the door.

"Summer, I need you to know something."

"Yes?"

"You're moving in with me tomorrow."

"Am I now?" she said with a smile.

"Yes. No arguments. I need to go now and catch up with Murray quickly. Get a drink and I'll meet you in the kitchen."

She kissed his lips softly and walked off. The arresting officers would sign Dotty Foster in while he stayed far away. The question was how long to stay away from the station.

The office was fairly quiet as he walked through to see Murray. Not as many people were working, but Murray was as usual. He knocked this time, and she yelled for him to come in.

He pushed open the door and prepared himself for her face to turn red with anger at the sight of him. To his surprise, she grinned at him for possibly the first time in his career. Her dark hair fell dishevelled around her shoulders, and a small glass of whiskey sat in front of her on the desk.

"I don't know what you're doing here, Alex Swanson. *But* she's coming home, so I'm happy regardless and you will not spoil my mood."

"Who's coming home?" he asked, bewildered at the sight of a happy, smiling Jane Murray.

"Hart! Good god, Swanson. What do you need anyway? Have you caused me any more trouble? You should be at home, you know."

Silence fell between them. She took a slow sip of her whiskey and watched him. He stood at the door with one hand resting against it awkwardly. This wasn't the Murray he knew. She was so chirpy.

"Why are you just standing there? Sit down," she barked.

That was more like it. He walked into the room and took a seat opposite her desk. The woody caramel scent of the whiskey drifted over to his nostrils. Her smile grew wider, and he almost felt guilty that he was about to bring her high down completely.

"What trouble have you caused me then?" she asked again. "Lay it on me."

"I arrested Dotty Foster."

Her smile disappeared, eyes closed. The familiar shade of red lightened her cheeks slightly, though there was no bulging vein. Her chest moved as she inhaled deeply before addressing him in a slow, measured voice.

"Swanson, you can't arrest people when you're under review for temporary suspension. You know this."

"She tried to stab Summer right in front of me with a huge carving knife. I asked a squad car to arrest her. I only held her until they got there. It was merely a citizen's arrest."

She sighed heavily and sat back in the chair. "Hmm. That changes things, I suppose."

"You don't look surprised that she tried to stab Summer."

"Nothing surprises me in this job. I've been doing it at least ten years longer than you. Are you surprised?"

He shrugged. "Yes, actually. A bit at least."

There was a knock at the door and their heads snapped around with a similar scowl.

"Yes?" Murray shouted.

The door opened slowly, and in walked the big brute of an officer who had placed the cuffs on Dotty Foster and pushed her into the back of the squad car. His name was Gary Wilsop. A gentle giant. He looked at Swanson like he'd rather be anywhere else in the world and cleared his throat before he spoke.

"Er, that lady we just arrested, Dotty Foster? She said she will only talk to you." He nodded at Swanson. "She reckons only you will understand her situation."

"Perfect." Swanson stood. He had a few choice words to say to Dotty Foster.

"Not so fast," Murray said. "Sit. You're involved. You can't interview her. I'm sick of these people demanding who they speak to. Does she have a legal representative with her?"

Gary nodded. "Well, they're on their way. Should be here within half an hour."

"Okay. We'll wait until they arrive and then I will interview her."

Swanson's face fell. "But—"

"You can watch the interview. Now piss off and have a cup of tea or something."

"I don't drink tea," he snapped.

"Just fuck off, Swanson. I need to think. You—" She pointed at poor Gary, who was still standing at the door. "You interview Summer Thomas. Make sure everything is above board. I have enough trouble with this idiot ruining things."

She pointed at Swanson, and he stood to leave. His eyes flicked to the glass of whiskey.

"Don't worry. I've only had a sip. Why did I think I'd have a chance for anything more than a sip? Off you go."

She shooed him away with both hands, and he followed Gary out of the office. The door closed behind them, and Gary gave him a look of pure relief.

"Go easy on Summer," Swanson warned him. "She's been through a lot."

"I will. Let me know what Foster says to her."

Swanson nodded, and Gary walked away. There was nothing else to do other than wait for Summer and Foster to be inter-viewed, so Swanson walked off to the kitchen. A heavy ball of emotion clutched at his chest, waiting to be released. He was another step closer. The answers were within reach. But he wasn't out of the woods yet. He couldn't relax until they were all arrested, including Lisa Trent and Ben Jackson.

34

Swanson

Half an hour later Summer was in an interview room with Gary making her statement, and Swanson leaned against the counter in the kitchen. He chugged down his second pint of water. The liquid was so cold he could feel it running all the way down his throat. He hadn't realised how dehydrated his tired body was until he started to drink.

Though he choked on the final glug as Murray's face appeared in the doorway. She came from nowhere and made him jump. He plonked the glass back on the side and spluttered water down his hoody, leaving a nice wet patch on the front.

"Christ, Swanson. I do worry about you. Now come on. You can watch the interview before you give your own statement. You'll only bug me with a million questions after it anyway, and I could do with your input on whatever she says. You know the case better than any of us."

She walked off, and he rushed out of the room to follow her. She disappeared into interview room two, and Swanson continued to the next door that held the screens for cameras in the interview room. The room was pretty small, and it was dark thanks to the fact that it had no windows. He didn't bother to flick the light on. The light from the six screens was enough to see what he was doing.

He took a seat on one of the two blue swivel chairs and watched the middle screen—the one that showed Dotty Foster on one side of the table with a pretentious-looking man in a black suit that he presumed to be her solicitor, and Murray on the other side sitting straight and looking scary. Murray hit the recording device and completed their introductions.

"I said I wanted to speak to Alex Swanson," Foster said roughly to Murray. Her posh accent from before had disappeared. What a fake.

"I am the closest you will get to Alex Swanson." Murray smiled. "I run his team and don't normally get involved in interviews, but this is a very important case, so you have my attention. For now."

"Oh. Okay." Dotty nodded as if impressed. "I will cooperate, of course. But I'll need some sort of protection against the people I need to mention in order to explain my actions tonight."

"You want to request witness protection?" Murray asked.

"Yes. There are some very dangerous people in this circle, and I need to make sure you will protect me."

Swanson scoffed. It was Summer who needed protection from her.

"Whether you are entitled to witness protection depends on what information you are about to tell me. If you are an innocent party and at risk because of your statement, then I can see what I can do for you. But according to my witness tonight, you followed and then tried to kill one of my own members of staff this morning."

"I had to!" Dotty screeched and then choked on a sob.

There were no tears, but Murray handed her a small packet of tissues from her pocket. Swanson rubbed the strands of his beard. Tissues were the last thing he would've given her for her fake tears.

"Here. It's okay. Tell me why you felt you had to hurt her."

Dotty shrugged. "I don't get told why. Only who."

"Tell me in more detail, Dotty, or this interview will end quickly."

Dotty lowered her head, pretending to sob into her chest.

"I think I just need a minute please."

"Of course," Murray replied.

She stopped the tape and the camera flicked off. The door to the interview room banged shut in the corridor outside, and he flew out of the camera room to meet her.

"Why did you give her a break so easily?"

"Because, stress head, I saw a text flash up about DNA."

Swanson leaned back against the wall. "DNA on what?"

"That glass you picked up from your poor aunt's house. It had DNA. The results are in, and it doesn't belong to Barb or her idiot son."

"Who then?"

"It belongs to Dorothy Tilly."

It took Swanson a second to process the name. Tilly. Dorothy Tilly. "*Dead* Dorothy Tilly?"

"Yes, Swanson. *Dead* Dorothy Tilly." Murray grinned. "And I know where she is."

"Where?"

"Wait and see."

He cursed as she disappeared back into the interview room

rather than just telling him. He rushed back into the camera room and stared at the screen as it turned back on. Dotty and her solicitor appeared again, as did Murray, who looked more smug than he'd ever seen her.

"Okay, Ms Tilly. Tell me from the beginning what happened."

Dotty Foster scoffed. "The beginning? We're talking years ago when I was just a young'un."

"So you are Dorothy, then. Dorothy Tilly. Nice to meet you."

Swanson's eyes nearly popped out of his head. He stood and paced the room. Dotty Foster was Dorothy Tilly. That's why there were no pictures of her body on file. The evil bitch was right in front of them the whole time.

Tilly's face reddened. She opened and closed her mouth like a fish. Her solicitor was flicking through notes.

"I was going to tell you!" Tilly stammered. "But like I said, these are some really scary people we're dealing with here. I will tell you everything from the beginning."

"Go on." Murray smiled encouragingly.

35

Swanson

S wanson gripped the edge of the chair. It took everything in him not to storm into the interview room and take over. He'd definitely lose his job then. It would be easier if he could have called Hart, or Summer, but they were both busy. Instead, he had to listen intently while Tilly talked Murray through what happened. Luckily, there was a notepad on the table in the camera room, and he grabbed it to write down his thoughts.

"As a foster kid I ended up being fostered by a cop and his wife." Tilly paused.

She sighed heavily and stared at the wall. It seemed she was bringing up some long forgotten and painful memories.

"Go on, Dorothy."

"The people that took me in weren't very nice people. We're talking a long time ago now when this happened. They didn't do the same checks they do these days. You have a million checks no matter what on foster and adoption families now. People don't even go for it anymore because it's too hard. But back then, you *police* especially were automatically trusted to be good people just because of your jobs. But they beat me and made me do everything around the house. They treated me like a slave, especially the man."

"What was his name?" Murray asked gently.

"The police officer? Paul Jackson. You won't find him. He's dead now. His own biological son killed him in the end."

Even Murray looked taken aback by that statement.

"His son killed him?" she asked.

"Yes. He's still alive. His name is Ben Jackson. He was a police officer as well, but he's retired. He's more evil than his dad ever was."

"So Paul Jackson had his own kids then. Why did he foster you?"

"He fostered lots of us. There were three of us when I lived there. Then another boy turned up just before I left. Mandy Harris was there with me. She was my foster sister."

"But why? If he had his own kids, who he didn't treat well, and had a well-paid job? It doesn't make much sense to me."

"He wanted his own little army to play with."

"An army? For what?"

"To torture until we bent to his every will."

Even on the camera feed Swanson could see the darkness in Tilly's eyes. As much as he knew she'd say anything to get out of going to prison, he believed every word when she talked about Paul Jackson.

"And what did he make them do?"

"Sometimes nothing. He just destroyed them and then kicked them out with nowhere to go. Other times we'd steal things for him from shops or from people. Sometimes he'd make us hurt people. He was a sick man."

"Is that why his son killed him?"

Tilly nodded gently. She sniffed and dabbed at her eyes. "Ben snapped one day when Paul was beating him, and he overpowered him. He did it with his bare hands. Strangled him to death. I saw the whole thing. I was only fifteen. It was terrifying."

"Was he arrested?"

"No. He blamed it on another kid. A big lad who was one of the foster lot. He made me be a witness and threatened to kill me if I didn't repeat the story he'd made up. Then Maria, Ben's mother, turned to drink. She did nothing except get drunk in her room every day. Ben ran that household. That family have had control of me my entire life."

"Talk me through how that links to what has happened today," Murray continued. "Why did you follow and attack this person?"

"I was so scared of Ben that I did everything he said. I did some awful things to the other kids so he wouldn't do them to me. I became his second in command. When he wasn't around, I was in charge of the house. If I'm honest, it was thrilling being in control after years of not having any. When I became an adult, Ben made me become a foster carer. He said I needed to carry it on; he threatened to kill me otherwise. Not in so many words, but I knew he'd killed more than just his dad. He got a thrill from the violence. He got me a beautiful house in the country."

"How did he afford that as a police officer?"

"The Jackson family always had money. I'm not sure specif-ically where it came from, but it wasn't just from his job. I think it was from the jobs he made the kids do sometimes. The stealing and hurting people, but he never explained it fully to me. When I got the house, I took a few kids in and tried to train them up how he wanted. He'd visit sometimes and make sure the kids were well-behaved and compliant. He'd roped in a social worker to bring us kids who had no family left. The ones who had already hurt people were suitable candidates if possible. Life was finally good for a few years. I had my own place. My own money. My own kids. But it all went wrong in the end."

"How so?"

"Men, typically. I met someone. His name was Trevor, and I fell madly in love. I got pregnant, and I wanted out. I wanted a normal life. He wanted me to get out. He didn't like the control Ben had over me or our lives. When Ben came round, we told him I was pregnant and would be moving away. We told him we wanted freedom." Her lip quivered, and she sucked in a breath.

"What did he say?" Murray asked softly.

Tilly took a deep breath. "He didn't say a word. He took out a knife, and killed Trevor right in front of me."

"I'm really sorry to hear that, Dorothy."

She collapsed into tears, and Murray pushed the packet of tissues closer to her. Murray could sound so empathetic when she wanted, but he could see her vein bulge. Swanson knew her better. She was baiting. Acting like a friendly cop who was going to help her. But she was too furious about Charlie Marsh to help this woman.

"He made me hide the body. Threatened to beat me so bad I'd lose the baby if I didn't cover it up. And that baby ended up being the death of the whole thing. She was wild, and no matter how much I beat her to keep her compliant and safe from Ben, she just pushed back. When I met someone new and fell in love again, she really went mad. At that time I had two foster kids. One was a daft little boy who did anything I asked. He was a bit slow. The other was a distant girl. She was damaged, that one. She reminded me of myself. The social worker reckoned she'd killed her own parents, and one day she killed the second love of my life."

She collapsed into tears again, and Murray gave her a moment to collect herself.

"Who was he?"

"Lee," Tilly replied sadly. "Lee Torrent. She stabbed him over and over. And that wasn't even the worst bit."

"Take your time," she reassured her. "What happened next?"

"My own daughter stabbed me too. As Lee lay there bleeding, I tried to help him. But she got me and stabbed me right here." Tilly pointed at her stomach.

Swanson took the opportunity to glance at her solicitor. His face was white as a sheet.

"I grabbed a nearby cushion and she mainly stabbed at that. She was in such a frenzy she thought it was me. But she did nearly kill me. Then all three of them ran off and I never saw the little bitch again or the other two. I rang Ben as I lay there bleeding, and he came to help. He laughed and said it was a hazard of the job. But he did help me and gave me a new identity. And he's held it over my head ever since."

"How so?"

"Take recent events. He knew how close Mandy and I were. She was my sister, always has been." Her face darkened as she looked up at Murray with hard eyes. "And that bastard killed my sister and tried to *frame* me."

"Why would he do that?"

"I'm old now and not much use to him. He's sick of paying for me and her, and wanted to get rid of us both, but rather than just kill me he wanted to play with me. That's what he does. They like to attribute blame to most people they kill, too. So suspicion doesn't arise about lots of missing people. His daughter's a police officer now. She's one of your lot! Did you know that?"

"Tell me." Murray's expression did not give anything away.

"Her name's Lisa. She has a different surname to her dad, though. I'm not sure what it is. She's been texting some officer to give him clues that lead to me when I hadn't even done anything wrong. They wanted to clear things up after what happened with some other foster old kids in the summer."

"Some other foster kids? Don't you know who died in the summer?" Murray asked.

Tilly's scrunched up her face. "What do you mean?"

"The foster kids in the summer died, other than Billy. Billy is locked away in a secure mental health facility. Charlie is dead. Does the name Marcie Livingstone ring any bells?"

"No? I've never heard of her."

"There's reason to believe she was your daughter, Ms TIlly."

Her lips set in a thin line, and her eyes narrowed. "I have no daughter. She's been dead to me since she stabbed me."

Swanson felt the tiny hairs on the back of his neck raise. This woman presented herself as innocent and blameless, but she was evil through and through.

Murray tried a different tactic. "What did Ben Jackson tell you about a recent murder?"

"Ben told me that he'd killed a police officer's mum or aunt to make sure the police came gunning for me. They've been texting the same officer hints and threats. They want me to take the blame and not Billy. He's too valuable to them in terms of taking the blame for anything that goes south. I'm not stupid, though. I know they wanted him to take the blame for the texts but they didn't realise how hard it would be to plant a phone on him. He's watched like a hawk. Lisa beat another officer up in broad daylight to antagonise this cop. None of it was me, I swear. I've never actually killed anyone. I'm not like him. I just tried to survive and help the foster kids to do the same."

"So you already knew Billy was in the secure unit then. Did you already know Marcie and Charlie were dead?

"I didn't know about them. I knew two women died, but not who they were." Her face remained devoid of emotion.

"You say you aren't like them. Yet you tried to stab a woman tonight. Why were you following her?"

"As I said, Ben likes to play games. He said he would lead the officer away from me and give me enough money to disappear if I stabbed this bitch. His words—"

That was it. The camera room door was open before Swanson realised what he was doing. He pushed open the interview room door. The three people within turned to look at him. Tilly stared at him with terrified, wide eyes. She recognised him instantly. He moved towards her, his fists clenched and breathing so heavily it was the only sound in the room. Murray stood quickly.

"Out please," she said in a voice that warranted no arguments.

Not that it got through to him. He took another step forward, the rage within him taking over any rational thought.

"Swanson!" Another voice from behind made him whip around.

Hart stood in the corridor with a crutch in her hand and an angry scowl on her face. She looked frail but furious. And he couldn't help but forget about Tilly for a second and smile at the angry woman in front of him.

"Get out here now."

Only then did it occur to him he was in the interview room about to hurt a *woman*, in front of her solicitor, his boss and a camera no less, and he finally did as he was told. Hart closed the interview room door shut behind him.

"I'm gone for three days and you're suddenly acting mad?" she snapped. Her right eye was seriously bruised, and his jaw clenched. Was it Tilly who beat her? Or Trent?

"You shouldn't even be at work," he snapped back, pointing to her face.

"I'm here to drop off a sick note, actually!"

"Yes. And find out what's going on, you nosy sod."

"Of course. Now come and tell me everything I've missed."

She turned away and headed to the camera room, and finally everything felt like it would be okay.

36

Summer

Swanson grabbed the last box from the removal van and lugged it through the front door and into Barb's office. *His* office. Though he might never get used to saying that. Aunt Barb was a wealthy woman who lived for her sons despite Swanson's feelings about them. She left them every penny—except for the house they rarely visited. Neither needed another large house. They'd also refused to speak to him since finding out. It was a win win.

Not that he would've kept the house if it wasn't for Summer and Joshua. It was the perfect family home in a beautiful area with fantastic schools. And certainly a better home than he could ever have provided for them. He stood back to rest his aching arms and admired the view as Summer bent over a box in the office. She pulled out a soft toy shaped like a husky dog and a football blanket.

"I'm going to sort Joshua's bedroom first, babe," she yelled as she stood up. She jumped when she saw him standing in the corner. "Shit! I didn't hear you come in. I'm going to do his room so he can sleep. Why are you lurking there?"

"I've just had some good news." He moved towards her and wrapped his arms around her shoulders. She sunk into his chest.

"And what might that be?" she asked.

"They've found Lisa Trent and Ben Jackson. They were holed up somewhere in Birmingham. Someone's bringing them to the station as we speak."

She pulled back and looked up at him. "So it's over? For sure this time?"

He shrugged and let go of her. "We'll find out soon, I suppose."

The pitter patter of small footsteps made them turn, and Joshua appeared in the doorway. His hair stuck up in different directions and his cheeks were bright red from excitement.

"This place is amazing!" he said as he ran towards them. To Swanson's surprise, he threw his skinny arms around his stomach first. He always went to Summer first. "Thanks, Alex!"

He turned and ran off without even looking at Summer, who laughed at Swanson's shocked expression.

"I think you're his favourite now." She smiled. "I'm not going to compete with this house!"

"Never," he replied. It was clear to anyone who met them that Joshua adored his mother. No one else came close.

"He has fallen for you just as much as I did," she said. "What will happen next with Trent and Jackson then? I still can't believe it was Trent."

"They'll be interviewed. Evidence gathered and so on. I'm staying well away from it all. I'm still on compassionate leave until next month and I'm not allowed to know anything more."

"So Hart will be around regularly to keep us updated while

I'm off work this week then?"

"Of course." He grinned back. "Let's crack on, then. We've got a lot to unpack. You sort Joshua's room and I'll sort ours so we have somewhere to sleep first."

"Yes, all right. You're not at work now. Stop giving me orders and bugger off."

She left the room, and he heard her soft footsteps going up the stairs. He turned and noticed behind the pile of boxes, Barb's desk still sat there. He removed a couple of boxes to make a path and ran his finger along the edge of the desk that had once meant so much to him. His forefinger touched the mark left by the murderer, which must have been Trent or Jackson. It should have been sent in for evidence, really. But clearly someone hadn't done their job properly. Mainly him.

Something else caught his eye behind the desk. The box of Christmas decorations and next to it, two neatly stacked Christmas presents. He picked them up gently and laid them on the desk. They could take pride of place under the tree this year.

He sighed and texted Hart about the desk. He could pick out a new one. Maybe a replica. Or a different one altogether. A fresh start was something they all needed, and now he had all the resources he needed to give Joshua and Summer the life they deserved thanks to Barb. Even after death, she looked out for him. And now he had his own family to do the same.

Thank you so much for reading The Revelation! Follow me on social media and let me know what you think.
Are you ready for more? Check out the next book in the series, You'll See, on Amazon now!

Also by Ashley Beegan

You'll See

Someone's been keeping secrets. They're about to be exposed.

Piper hoped moving back to her hometown would be the fresh start she needed after her boss was murdered right in front of her. It meant a new job, a quiet life, and time to heal from the losses that have scarred her. Her boyfriend, Adam, is up for the move too. But working at a mental health home is anything but quiet, and her long-buried childhood memories begin to resurface.

Then the letters start arriving.

At first, they seem harmless, almost protective. But as they grow darker and more intrusive, Piper realises someone is watching her. They know her secrets, her routines, even her thoughts. They don't like the people around her, and they aren't afraid to make that clear.

Detective Inspector Alex Swanson and pregnant forensic psychologist Summer Thomas are determined to help, but as Piper's grip on reality begins to falter, she struggles to untangle the web of lies surrounding her. With her stalker always one step ahead, she's forced to confront not only the ghosts of her past but the shocking truth about the people closest to her.

The danger is far closer than Piper ever imagined, and someone is willing to do whatever it takes to keep her under their control.

The Holiday Home

The beautiful, old cottage in the Peak District was the perfect place for Simone to take a much-needed break following a horrific attack. Surrounded by nature and peace, she can finally relax.

Until she realises she isn't alone.

Someone is hiding in the woods, and sneaking inside to leave her unwanted surprises. Her therapist, Theo, insists there is nobody else there, other than the gardener, and she just needs to rest. But as she grows closer to Theo, Simone finds out that this particular cabin has some dark secrets.

Secrets that people will **kill** to protect.

Printed in Great Britain
by Amazon